"Tell me about this job you'd like me to do for you."

He didn't owe her for her signature on their divorce papers, but if by doing this he could end things between them on a more pleasant note, then perhaps he'd find the closure he so desperately needed. "And, yes, you have my word that I will never reveal to another soul what you're about to tell me, unless you give me leave to."

She stared at him as if trying to sum him up. With a start he realized she was trying to decide whether to trust him or not. "You don't trust my word of honor?"

"If you were after any kind of revenge on me, what I'm about to tell you would provide you with both the means and the method."

He didn't want revenge. He'd never wanted revenge. He just wanted to move on with his life.

And to kiss her.

Dear Reader,

There's something about a reunion story that sings to my soul—both as a reader and as a writer. There's so much angst and history to explore. When an estranged couple who once loved each other to distraction come face-to-face after a number of years apart, the discord and antipathy can be powerful and immediate. That might be why reunion stories are one of my all-time favorite romance tropes.

The characters of Caro and Jack have been with me for years, so I'm pleased I finally had the chance to write their story. I sent them on a wild ride—there are hijinks and escapades—with high stakes and blistering emotion. Still, as this *is* my twentieth Harlequin Romance story, that only seemed fair. :)

Can you tell yet that I had a blast writing this book? I hope you have just as much fun reading it.

Hugs,

Michelle

A Deal to Mend Their Marriage

Michelle Douglas

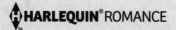

Recycling programs
for this product may
not exist in your area.

ISBN-13: 978-0-373-74374-2

A Deal to Mend Their Marriage

First North American Publication 2016

Copyright © 2016 by Michelle Douglas

Printed in U.S.A.

www.Harlequin.com

Michelle Douglas has been writing for Harlequin since 2007 and believes she has the best job in the world. She lives in a leafy suburb of Newcastle, on Australia's east coast, with her own romantic hero, a house full of dust and books, and an eclectic collection of '60s and '70s vinyl. She loves to hear from readers and can be contacted via her website, michelle-douglas.com.

Books by Michelle Douglas

Harlequin Romance

The Vineyards of Calanetti

Reunited by a Baby Secret

The Wild Ones

Her Irresistible Protector
The Rebel and the Heiress

Bellaroo Creek!

The Cattleman's Ready-Made Family

Mothers in a Million

First Comes Baby

The Man Who Saw Her Beauty
Bella's Impossible Boss
The Nanny Who Saved Christmas
The Redemption of Rico D'Angelo
Road Trip with the Eligible Bachelor
Snowbound Surprise for the Billionaire
The Millionaire and the Maid

Visit the Author Profile page
at Harlequin.com for more titles.

For Greg, who brings me glasses of red wine whenever I need them and supplies hugs on demand—the benchmarks of a romantic hero. :)

CHAPTER ONE

THE FIRST PRICKLE of unease wormed through Caro when the lawyer's gaze slid from her to Barbara and then down to the papers in front of him—her father's will, presumably. The lawyer picked up a pen, turned it over several times before setting it back to the table. He adjusted his tie, cleared his throat.

Even Barbara noticed his unwillingness to start proceedings. Turning ever so slightly, her step-mother reached out to pat Caro's hand. 'Caro, darling, if your father has disinherited you—'

Caro forced a laugh. 'There'll be no *if* about that, Barbara.'

It was a given, and they both knew it. Caro just wanted all the unpleasantness over so she could put it behind her. Her father was about to utter the last words he ever would to her—albeit on paper. She had no expectation that they'd be any kinder in death than they had been in life.

'Mr Jenkins?' She prodded the lawyer with the

most pleasant smile she could muster. 'If you'd be so kind as to start we'd both appreciate it. Unless—' she pursed her lips '—we're waiting for someone else?'

'No, no one else.'

Mr Jenkins shook his head and Caro had to bite back a smile when the elderly lawyer's gaze snagged on the long, lean length of Barbara's legs, on display beneath her short black skirt. At thirty-seven—only seven years older than Caro—Barbara had better legs than Caro could ever hope to have. Even if she spent every waking hour at the gym and resisted every bit of sugar, butter and cream that came her way—which, of course, she had no intention of doing.

The lawyer shook himself. 'Yes, of course, Ms Fielding. We're not waiting for anyone else.'

'Come now,' she chided. 'You've known me my entire life. If you can't bring yourself to call me Caro, then surely you can call me Caroline?'

He sent her an agonised glance.

She made her smile gentle. 'I *am* prepared, you know. I fully expect that my father has disinherited me.'

She didn't add that the money didn't matter. Neither Mr Jenkins nor Barbara would believe her. The fact remained, though, that it had never been money she'd craved but her father's approval, his acceptance.

Her temples started to throb. With a superhuman effort she kept the smile on her face. 'I promise not to shoot the messenger.'

The lawyer slumped in what had been until recently her father's chair. He pulled off his spectacles and rubbed the bridge of his nose. 'You have it all wrong, Caro.'

Barbara clasped her hands together and beamed. 'I *knew* he wouldn't disinherit you!'

The relief—and, yes, the delight—on Barbara's face contrasted wildly with the weariness in Mr Jenkins's eyes. Cold fingers crept up Caro's spine. A premonition of what, exactly...?

Mr Jenkins pushed his spectacles back to his nose and folded his hands in front of him. 'There are no individual letters I need to deliver. There are no messages I need to pass on nor any individual bequests to run through. I don't even need to read out the will word for word.'

'Then maybe—' Barbara glanced at Caro '—you'd be kind enough to just give us the general gist.'

He slumped back and heaved out a sigh. 'Mr Roland James Philip Fielding has left all of his worldly goods—all of his wealth and possessions—to...'

Caro braced herself.

'Ms Caroline Elizabeth Fielding.'

It took a moment for the import of the lawyer's words to hit her. When they did, Caro had to grip the arms of her chair to counter the roaring in her ears and the sudden tilting of the room. Her father had left everything...*to her*? Maybe...maybe he'd loved her after all.

She shook her head. 'There must be a mistake.'

'No mistake,' the lawyer intoned.

'But surely there's a caveat that I can only inherit if I agree to administer my mother's trust?'

Her father had spent the last twenty years telling her it was her duty, her responsibility...her *obligation* to manage the charity he'd created in homage to her mother. Caro had spent those same twenty years refusing the commission.

Her father might have thought it was the sole reason Caro had been put on this earth, but she'd continued to dispute that sentiment right up until his death. She had no facility for figures and spreadsheets, no talent nor desire to attend endless board meetings and discuss the pros and cons of where the trust money should be best spent. She did not have a business brain and had no desire whatsoever to develop one. Simply put, she had no intention of being sacrificed on some altar of duty. End of story.

'No caveat.'

The lawyer could barely meet her eye. Her mind spun...

She shot to her feet, a hard ball lodging in her chest. 'What about Barbara?'

He passed a hand across his eyes. 'I'm afraid no

provision has been made for Mrs Barbara Fielding in the will.'

But that made no sense!

She spun to her stepmother. Barbara rose to her feet, her face pinched and white. Her eyes swam but not a single tear fell, and that was somehow worse than if she'd burst into noisy weeping and wailing.

'He doesn't make even a single mention of me?'

The lawyer winced and shook his head.

'But...but I did everything I could think of to make him happy. Did he never love me?' She turned to Caro. 'Was it all a lie?'

'We'll work something out,' Caro promised, reaching out to take Barbara's hand.

But the other woman wheeled away. 'We'll do nothing of the sort! We'll do exactly as your father wished!'

Barbara turned and fled from the room. Caro made to follow her—how could her father have treated his young wife so abominably?—but the lawyer called her back.

'I'm afraid we're not done.'

She stilled and then spun back, swallowing a sense of misgiving. 'We're not?'

'Your father instructed that I give you this.' He held out an envelope.

'But you said...'

'I was instructed to give this to you only after the reading of the will. And only in privacy.'

She glanced back at the door. Praying that Barbara wouldn't do anything foolish, she strode across and took the envelope. She tore it open and read the mercifully brief missive inside. She could feel her lips thinning to a hard line. She moistened them. 'Do you know what this says?'

After a short hesitation, he nodded. 'Your father believed Mrs Fielding was stealing from him. Valuables have apparently gone missing and...'

And her father had jumped to conclusions.

Caro folded the letter and shoved it into her purse. 'Items may well have gone missing, but I don't believe for one moment that Barbara is responsible.'

Mr Jenkins glanced away, but not before she caught the expression in his eyes.

'I know what people think about my father and his wife, Mr Jenkins. They consider Barbara a trophy wife. They think she only married my father for his money.'

He'd had *so much* money. Why cut Barbara out of his will when he'd had so much? Even if she *had* taken the odd piece of jewellery why begrudge it to her?

Damn him to hellfire and fury for being such a control freak!

'She *was* significantly younger than your father...'

By thirty-one years.

'That doesn't make her a thief, Mr Jenkins. My father was a difficult man and he was lucky to have Barbara. She did everything in her not insignificant powers to humour him and make him happy. What's more, I believe she was faithful to him for the twelve years they were married and I don't believe she stole from him.'

'Of course you know her better than I do—but, Miss Caroline, you do have a tendency to see the best in people.'

She'd been hard-pressed to see the best in her father. She pushed that thought aside to meet the lawyer's eyes. 'If Barbara did marry my father for his money believe me: she's earned every penny of it several times over.'

Mr Jenkins obviously thought it prudent to remain silent on the subject.

'If my father's estate has passed completely to me, then I can dispose of it in any way that I see fit, yes?'

'That's correct.'

Fine. She'd sell everything and give Barbara half. Even half was more than either one of them would ever need.

Half an hour later, after she'd signed all the relevant paperwork, Caro strode into the kitchen.

Dennis Paul, her father's butler, immediately shot to his feet.

'Let me make you a pot of tea, Miss Caroline.'

She kissed his cheek and pushed him back into his seat. 'I'll make the tea, Paul.' He insisted she call him Paul rather than Dennis. 'Please just tell me there's cake.'

'There's an orange syrup cake at the back of the pantry.'

They sipped tea and ate cake in silence for a while. Paul had been in her father's employ for as long as Caro could remember. He was more like an honorary uncle than a member of staff, and she found herself taking comfort in his quiet presence.

'Are you all right, Miss Caroline?'

'You *can* call me Caro you know.' It was an old argument.

'You'll always be Miss Caroline to me.' He grinned. 'Even though you're all grown up—married, no less, and holding a director's position at that auction house of yours.'

In the next instance his expression turned stricken. 'I'm sorry. I didn't mean to mention that bit about you being married. It was foolish of me.'

She shrugged and tried to pretend that the word *married* didn't burn through her with a pain that could still cripple her at unsuspecting moments. As she and Jack had been separated for the last five years, 'married' hardly seemed the right word to describe them. Even if, technically, it was true.

She forced herself to focus on something else instead. 'It's not *my* auction house, Paul. I just work there.'

She pulled in a breath and left off swirling her fork though the crumbs remaining on her plate.

'My father has left me everything, Paul. *Everything.*'

Paul's jaw dropped. He stared at her and then sagged back in his chair. 'Well, I'll be…'

His astonishment gratified her. At least she wasn't the only one shocked to the core at this turnaround. To describe her relationship with her father as 'strained' would be putting it mildly. And kindly.

He straightened. 'Oh, that *is* good news Miss Caroline. In more than one way.' He beamed at her, patting his chest just above his heart, as if urging it to slow its pace. 'I'm afraid I've a bit of confession to make. I've been squirrelling away odd bits and pieces here and there. Things of value, but nothing your father would miss, you understand. I just thought… Well, I thought you might need them down the track.'

Good grief! Paul was her father's thief?

Dear Lord, if he knew her father had written Barbara out of his will, thinking her the guilty party... *Oh!* And if Barbara knew what Paul had done...

Caro closed her eyes and tried to contain a shudder.

'Paul, you could've gone to jail if my father had ever found out what you were doing!'

'But there's no harm done now, is there? I mean, now that you've inherited the estate I don't need to find a way to...to get those things to you. They're legally yours.' His smile faded. 'Are you upset with me?'

How could she be? Nobody had ever gone out on a limb like that for her before. 'No, just... frightened at what might've happened,' she lied.

'You don't have to worry about those sorts of what-ifs any more.'

Maybe not, but she still had to find a way to make this right. 'It's only fair that I split the estate with Barbara.'

A breath shuddered out of him. He glanced around the kitchen pensively. 'Does that mean selling the old place?'

What on earth did she need with a mansion in Mayfair? She didn't say that out loud. This had been Paul's home for over thirty years. It hit her then that her father had made no provision in his will for Paul either. She'd remedy that as soon as she could.

'I don't know, Paul, but we'll work something

out. I'm not going to leave you high and dry, I promise. Trust me. You, Barbara and I—we're family.'

He snorted. 'Funny kind of family.'

She opened her mouth and then closed it, nodding. Never had truer words been spoken.

'Will you be staying the night, Miss Caro?'

Heavens, where Paul was concerned, *Miss Caro* was positively gushing—a sign of high sentiment and emotion.

From somewhere she found a smile. 'Yes, I think I'd better.' She had her own room in the Mayfair mansion, even though she rented a tiny one-bedroom flat in Southwark. 'Hopefully Barbara will… Well, hopefully I'll get a chance to talk to her.'

Hopefully she'd get a chance to put the other woman's mind at rest—at least about her financial future.

'Mrs Fielding refuses to join you for breakfast,' Paul intoned ominously the next morning as Caro helped herself to coffee.

Caro heaved back a sigh. Barbara had refused to speak to her at all last night. She'd tried calling out assurances to her stepmother through her closed bedroom door, but had given up when Barbara had started blasting show tunes—her father's favourites—from her music system.

'You will, however, be pleased to know that she did get up at some stage during the night to make herself something to eat.'

That was something at least.

'Oh, Miss Caroline! *You* need to eat something before you head off to work,' he said when she pushed to her feet.

'I'm fine, Paul, I promise.' Her appetite would eventually return. Although if he'd offered her cake for breakfast...

Stop thinking about cake.

'I'm giving Freddie Soames a viewing of a rather special snuffbox this morning.' She'd placed it in her father's safe—*her* safe—prior to the reading of the will yesterday. 'After that I'll take the rest of the day off and see if I can't get Barbara to talk to me then.'

As a director of Vertu, the silver and decorative arts division at Richardson's, one of London's leading auction houses, she had some flexibility in the hours she worked.

She glanced over her shoulder at Paul, who followed on her heels as she entered her father's study—*her* study. 'You *will* keep an eye on Barbara this morning, won't you?'

'If you wish it.'

She bit back a grin, punching in the combination to the safe. Ever since Paul had caught Barbara tossing the first Mrs Fielding's portrait into a closet, he'd labelled her as trouble. 'I *do* wish it.'

The door to the safe swung open and—Caro blinked, squinted and then swiped her hand through the empty space.

Her heart started to pound. 'Paul, please tell me I'm hallucinating.' Her voice rose. 'Please tell me the safe isn't empty.'

He moved past her to peer inside. 'Dear God in heaven!' He gripped the safe's door. 'Do you think we've been burgled?'

Something glittered on the floor at her feet. She picked it up. The diamond earing dangled from her fingers and comprehension shot through her at the same moment it spread across Paul's face.

'Barbara,' she said.

And at the same time he said, 'Mrs Fielding.'

She patted her racing heart. 'That's okay, then.'

'She'll have been after those jewels.'

'She's welcome to those jewels, Paul. They're hers. Father gave me Mother's jewels when I turned twenty-one.'

He harrumphed.

'But I really, *really* need that snuffbox back—this instant.'

She sped up to Barbara's first-floor bedroom, Paul still hot on her heels. She tapped on the door. 'Barbara?'

'Not now, Caro. Please, just leave me in peace.'

'I won't take up more than a moment of your time.' Caro swallowed. 'It's just that something has gone missing from the safe.'

'That jewellery is *mine*!'

'Yes, I know. I'm not referring to the jewellery.'

The door cracked open, and even the way Barbara's eyes flashed couldn't hide how red they were from crying. Caro's heart went out to the other woman.

'Are you accusing me of stealing something? Are you calling me a *thief*?'

'Of course not.' Caro tried to tamp down on the panic threatening to rise through her. 'Barbara, that jewellery belongs to you—I'm not concerned about the jewellery. Yesterday I placed a small item in the safe—a silver and enamel snuffbox about so big.' She held her hands about three inches apart to indicate the size. 'I have to show it to a potential buyer in an hour.'

Barbara tossed her hair. 'I didn't see any such thing and I certainly didn't take it.'

'I'm not suggesting for a moment that you did—not on purpose—but it's possible it was accidentally mixed in with the jewellery.' Behind her back she crossed her fingers. 'I'm *really* hoping it was. Would you mind checking for me?'

Barbara swept the door open and made a melodramatic gesture towards the bed. 'Take a look for yourself. *That's* what I took from the safe.'

The bed didn't look as if it had been slept in. Caro moved tentatively into the room to survey the items spread out on the bed. There was a diamond choker, a string of pearls, a sapphire pendant and assorted earrings and pins, but no snuffbox. Her heart hammered up into her throat.

'It's not here,' Paul said, leaning over to scan the items.

Caro concentrated on not hyperventilating. 'If… if I don't find that snuffbox I'll…I'll lose my job.'

Not just her job but her livelihood. She'd never get another job in the industry for as long as she lived. In all likelihood legal action would be taken. She'd—

Breathe! Don't forget to breathe.

Barbara dumped the contents of her handbag onto the bed and then slammed her hands on her hips. 'Once and for all—I haven't taken your rotten snuffbox! Would you like to search the entire room?'

Yes! Though of course she wouldn't.

Her gaze landed on a tiny framed photograph of her father that had spilled from Barbara's bag. An ache opened up in her chest. How could he have treated Barbara so badly? She understood Barbara's anger and disappointment, her hurt and disillusionment, but she would never do anything to intentionally hurt *her*—of that Caro was certain. She just needed to give the other woman a chance to calm down, cool off...think rationally.

'Did you not sleep at all last night, Barbara?'

Barbara's bottom lip wobbled, but she waved to the chaise lounge. 'I didn't want to sleep in the bed that I shared with...'

Caro seized her hands. 'He loved you, you know.'

'I don't believe you. Not after yesterday.'

'I mean to split the estate with you—fifty-fifty.'

'It's not what *he* wanted.'

'He was an idiot.'

'You shouldn't speak about him that way.' Barbara retrieved her hands. 'If you're finished here...?'

'Will you promise to have dinner with me tonight?'

'If I say yes, will you leave me in peace until then?'

'Absolutely.'

'Yes.'

Caro and Paul returned to the study to search the room, in case the snuffbox had fallen during Barbara's midnight raid on the safe, but they didn't find anything—not even the partner to that diamond earring.

'You didn't take it by any chance, did you, Paul?'

'No, Miss Caroline.'

'I'm sorry. I thought I'd just check, seeing as...'

'No offence taken, Miss Caroline.' He pursed

his lips. '*She* has it, you know. I'm not convinced that the second Mrs Fielding is a nice lady. I once saw her throw your mother's portrait into a closet, you know.'

Caro huffed out a sigh. 'Well… I, for one, like her.'

'What are you going to do?'

She needed time. Pulling her phone from her purse, she rang her assistant.

'Melanie, a family emergency has just come up. Could you please ring Mr Soames and reschedule his viewing for later in the week?'

The later the better! She didn't add that out loud, though. She didn't want to alert anyone to the fact that something was wrong—that she'd managed to lose a treasure.

Her assistant rang back a few minutes later. 'Mr Soames is flying out to Japan tomorrow. He'll be back Thursday next week. He had asked if you'd be so good as to meet with him the following Friday morning at ten o'clock.'

'No problem at all. Pop it in my diary.'

Friday was ten days away. She had ten days to put this mess to rights.

She seized her purse and made for the door. Paul still trailed after her. 'What do you mean to do, Miss Caroline?'

She wanted to beg him not to be so formal. 'I need to duck back to my flat and collect a few things, drop in at work to pick up my work diary and apply for a few days' leave. Then I'll be back. I'll be staying for a few days.'

'Very good, Miss Caroline.'

She turned in the entrance hall to face him, but before she'd swung all the way around her gaze snagged on a photograph on one of the hall tables. *A photograph of her and Jack.*

For a moment the breath jammed in her throat. She pointed. 'Why?' she croaked.

Paul clasped his hands behind his back. 'This house belongs to you now, Miss Caroline. It seemed only right that you should have your things around you.'

Her heart cramped so tightly she had to fight for breath. 'Yes, perhaps… But…not that photo, Paul.'

'I always liked Mr Jack.'

'So did I.'

But Jack had wanted to own her—just as her father had wanted to own her. And, just like her father, Jack had turned cold and distant when she'd refused to submit to his will. And then he'd left.

Five years later a small voice inside her still taunted her with the sure knowledge that she'd have been happier with Jack on *his* terms than she was now on her own terms, as her own woman. She waved a hand in front of her face. That was a ridiculous fairytale—a fantasy with no basis in reality. She and Jack were always going to end in tears. She could see that now.

Very gently, Paul reached out and placed the photograph facedown on the table. 'I'm sure there must be a nice photograph of you and your mother somewhere.'

She snapped back to the present, trying to push the past firmly behind her. 'See if you can find a photo of me and Barbara.'

Paul rolled his eyes in a most un-butler-like fashion and Caro laughed and patted his arm.

'The things I ask of you…'

He smiled down at her. 'Nothing's too much trouble where you're concerned, Miss Caro.'

She glanced up the grand staircase towards the first-floor rooms.

'I'll keep an eye on Mrs Fielding,' he added. 'I'll try to dissuade her if she wants to go out. If she insists, I'll send one of the maids with her.' He glanced at the grandfather clock. 'They're due to come in and start cleaning any time now.'

'Thank you.' She didn't want Barbara doing anything foolish—like trying to sell that snuff-box if she *did* have it. 'I'll be as quick as I can.'

Despite the loss of the snuffbox and all the morning's kerfuffle, it was Jack's face that rose in her mind and memories of the past that invaded Caro, chasing her other concerns aside, as she trudged across Westminster Bridge.

The sight of that photograph had pulled her up short. They'd been so happy.

For a while.

A very brief while.

So when she first saw his face in the midst of the crowd moving towards her on the bridge, Caro dismissed it as a flight of fancy, a figment of her imagination. Until she realised that blinking hadn't made the image fade. It had only made the features of that face clearer—a face that was burned onto her soul.

She stopped dead. Jack was in London?

The crowd surged around her, but she couldn't move. All she could do was stare.

Jack! Jack! Jack!

His name pounded at her as waves of first cold and then heat washed over her. The ache to run to him nearly undid her. And then his gaze landed on her and he stopped dead too.

She couldn't see the extraordinary cobalt blue of his eyes at this distance, but she recognised the way they narrowed, noted the way his nostrils flared. She'd always wondered what would happen if they should accidentally meet on the street. Walking past each other without so much as an acknowledgment obviously wasn't an option, and she was fiercely glad about that.

Hauling in a breath, she tilted her head to the left a fraction and started towards the railing of the bridge. She leaned against it, staring down at the brown water swirling in swift currents below. He came to stand beside her, but she kept her gaze on the water.

'Hello, Jack.'

'Caro.'

She couldn't look at him. Not yet. She stared at the Houses of Parliament and then at the facade of the aquarium on the other side of the river. 'Have you been in London long?'

'No.'

Finally she turned to meet his gaze, and her heart tried to grow bigger and smaller in the same moment. She read intent in his eyes and slowly straightened. 'You're here to see me?'

His demeanour confirmed it, but he nodded anyway. 'Yes.'

'I see.' She turned to stare back down at the river. 'Actually...' She frowned and sent him a sidelong glance. 'I don't see.'

He folded his tall frame and leaned on the railing, too. She dragged her gaze from his strong, hawk-like profile, afraid that if she didn't she might reach across and kiss him.

'I heard about your father.'

She pursed her lips, her stomach churning like the currents below. 'You didn't send a card.'

He didn't say anything for a moment. 'You send me a Christmas card every year...'

He never sent her one.

'Do you send *all* your ex-lovers Christmas cards?'

She straightened. 'Only the ones I marry.'

They both flinched at her words.

In the next moment she swung to him. 'Oh, please, let's not do this.'

'Do what?'

'Be mean to each other.'

He relaxed a fraction. 'Suits me.'

She finally looked at him properly and a breath eased out of her. She reached out to clasp his upper arm. She'd always found it incredibly difficult not to touch him. Through the fine wool of his suit jacket, she recognised his strength and the firm, solid feel of him.

'You look good, Jack—really good. I'm glad.'

'Are you?'

'Of course.' She squeezed his arm more firmly. 'I only ever wanted your happiness.'

'That's not exactly true, though—is it, Caro?'

Her hand fell away, back to her side.

'My happiness wasn't more important to you than your career.'

She pursed her lips and gave a nod. 'So you still blame me, then?'

'Completely,' he said without hesitation. 'And bitterly.'

She made herself laugh. 'Honesty was never our problem, was it?' But the unfairness of his blame burned through her. 'Why have you come to see me?'

He hauled in a breath, and an ache started up in the centre of her. 'Hearing about your father's death...' He glanced at her. 'Should I give you my condolences?'

She gave a quick shake of her head, ignoring the burn of tears at the backs of her eyes. Pretending her relationship with her father had been anything other than cold and combative would be ridiculous—especially with Jack.

'You don't miss him?'

His curiosity surprised her. 'I miss the *idea* of him.' She hadn't admitted that to another living soul. 'Now that he's gone there's no chance that our relationship can be fixed, no possibility of our differences being settled.' She lifted her chin. 'I didn't know I still harboured such hopes until after he died.'

Those blue eyes softened for a moment, and it felt as if the sun shone with a mad midday warmth rather than afternoon mildness.

'I am sorry for that,' he said.

She glanced away and the chill returned to the air. 'Thank you.'

The one thing the men in her life had in common

was their inability to compromise. She couldn't forget that.

'So, hearing about my father's death…?' she prompted.

He enunciated his next words very carefully and she could almost see him weighing them.

'It started me thinking about endings.'

Caro flinched, throwing up her arm as if to ward off a blow. She couldn't help it.

'For pity's sake, Caro!' He planted his legs. 'This *can't* come as a surprise to you.'

He was talking about divorce, and it shouldn't come as a shock, but a howling started up inside her as something buried in a deep, secret place cracked, breaking with a pain she found hard to breathe through.

'Are you going to faint?'

Anger laced his words and it put steel back in her spine. 'Of course not.'

She lifted her chin, still struggling for breath as the knowledge filtered through her that just as she'd harboured secret hopes of reconciling with her father, so she had harboured similar hopes where Jack was concerned.

Really? How could you be so…optimistic?

She waved a hand in front of her face. The sooner those hopes were routed and dashed, the better. She would *never* trust this man with her heart again.

She lifted her chin another notch against the anger in his eyes. 'You'll have to forgive me. It's been something of a morning. We had the reading of my father's will yesterday. Things have been a little...fraught since.'

He rubbed a fist across his mouth, his eyes hooded. 'I'm sorry. If I'd known, I'd have given you another few weeks before approaching you with this.' His anger had faded but a hardness remained. His lips tightened as he glanced around. 'And I should've found a better place to discuss the issue than in the middle of Westminster Bridge.'

She had a feeling her reaction would have been the same, regardless of the where or when. 'You've just been to my flat?' she asked.

He nodded. 'I was going to catch the tube up to Bond Street.' It was the closest underground station to where she worked. 'But...'

'But the Jubilee Line is closed due to a suspicious package at Green Park Station,' she finished for him. It was why she was walking. That and the need for fresh air. 'I'm on my way to the flat now. We can walk. Or would you prefer to take a cab?'

Jack didn't like Caro's pallor. Rather than answer verbally, he hailed a passing cab and bundled her into it before the motorists on the bridge could start tooting their horns. The sooner this was over, the better.

Caro gave the driver her address and then settled in her seat and stared out of the side window. He did the same on his side of the cab, but he didn't notice the scenery. What rose up in his mind's eye was the image of Caro when he'd first laid eyes on her—and the punching need to kiss her that had almost overwhelmed him. A need that lingered with an off-putting urgency.

He gritted his teeth against it and risked a glance at her. She'd changed.

It's been five years, pal, what did you expect?

He hadn't expected to want her with the same ferocity now as he had back then.

He swallowed. She'd developed more gloss... more presence. She'd put on a bit of weight and it suited her. Five years ago he'd thought her physically perfect, but she looked even better now and every hormone in his body hollered that message out, loud and clear.

After five years his lust should have died a natural death, surely? If not that then it should at least have abated.

Hysterical laughter sounded in the back of his mind.

Caro suddenly swung to him and he prayed to God that he hadn't made some noise that had betrayed him.

'I hear you're running your own private investigation agency these days?'

'You hear correctly.'

Gold gleamed in the deep brown depths of her eyes. 'I hear it's very successful?'

'It's doing okay.'

A hint of a smile touched her lips. She folded her arms and settled back in her seat.

'Calculating the divorce settlement already, Caro?'

Very slowly her smile widened, and his traitorous heart thumped in response.

'Something like that,' she purred. 'Driver?' She leaned forward. 'Could you let us out at the bakery just up here on the right? I need to buy cake.'

Cake? The Caro he knew didn't eat *cake*.

The Caro you knew was a figment of your imagination!

CHAPTER TWO

'JACK, I FIND myself in a bit of a pickle.'

Caro set a piece of cake on the coffee table in front of him, next to a steaming mug of coffee. She'd chosen a honey roll filled with a fat spiral of cream and dusted with glittering crystals of sugar.

Jack stared at it and frowned. 'Money?'

'No, not money.'

He picked up his coffee and glanced around. Her flat surprised him. It was so *small*. Still, it was comfortable. Her clothes weren't cheap knock-offs either. No, Caro looked as quietly opulent as ever.

She perched on the tub chair opposite him. 'You seem a little hung up on the money issue.'

Maybe because when they'd first met he hadn't had any. At least not compared to Caro's father.

Don't forget she was disinherited the moment she married you.

She hadn't so much as blinked an eye at the time. She'd said it didn't matter. She'd said that given her and her father's adversarial relationship it was inevitable. And he'd believed her.

He bit back a sigh. Who knew? Maybe she'd even believed the lie back then.

'Perhaps we should clear that issue up first,' she continued.

'You didn't have to buy cake on my account, you know.'

He wished she hadn't. Her small acts of courtesy had always taken him off guard and left him all at sea. They'd oozed class and made it plain that she'd had an education in grace and decorum—one that he'd utterly lacked. It had highlighted all the differences between them. He'd lived in fear of unknowingly breaking one of those unknown rules of hers and hurting her.

You hurt her anyway.

And she'd hurt him.

He pushed those thoughts away.

Caro gazed at him and just for a fraction of a second her lips twitched. 'I didn't buy cake on *your* account.'

She forked a mouthful of honey roll to her lips and while she didn't actually close her eyes in relish, he had a feeling that deep inside herself she did.

'This cake is very good. Jean-Pierre is a wizard.'

That must be the baker's name. She'd always

taken pains to find out and then use people's names. He'd found that charming. Once. Now he saw it for what it was—a front.

'But if you don't want it please don't eat it.'

He leaned towards her, his frown deepening. 'You never used to eat cake.'

'I know! I can't believe what I was missing.' Her eyes twinkled for a moment and her lips lifted, but then she sobered and her face became void of emotion. 'But people change. Five years ago you wouldn't have been at all concerned with the threat of me taking you for half of all you owned.'

He'd worked hard during the last five years to make a success of his security and private investigation firm. Such a success, in fact, that if he were still alive even Caro's father would sit up and take notice. He sat back. It seemed he'd been making money while Caro had been eating cake. It summed them up perfectly.

'Five years ago I didn't have anything worth taking, Caro.'

She looked as if she might disagree with him, but after a moment she simply shook her head. 'Let me waste no further time in putting your mind at rest. I don't want your money, Jack. I never did. You should know that yesterday I was named as my father's sole beneficiary.'

Whoa! He straightened. Okay…

'As we're still married I expect you could make a successful claim on the estate. Do you wish to?'

His hands clenched to fists. 'Absolutely not!'

She shrugged and ate more cake. '*You* haven't changed that much, then. Earlier today I'd have staked the entire estate on you not wanting a penny.'

Damn straight! But her odd belief in him coupled with her utter lack of concern that he could have taken her for a financial ride pricked him. 'So, this *pickle* you're in?'

She set her plate down, clasping her hands to her knees. 'Jack, I'd like to hire you for a rather... delicate job.'

He tried to hide his shock.

'But before we continue I'd like an assurance of your discretion and confidentiality.'

'You wouldn't have asked me that once.' She'd have taken it for granted.

'True, but when you walked away from our marriage you proved my trust in you was misplaced. So I'm asking for an assurance now.'

He glanced down to find his knuckles had turned white. He unclenched his hands and took a deep breath. 'I should warn you that if this "delicate" matter of yours involves murder or threats of violence then I'm honour-bound to—'

'Don't be ridiculous! Of course it doesn't. Don't

take me for a fool. I'm a lot of things, but I'm not a fool.'

He bit back something very rude. Bending down, he pulled the divorce papers he'd had drawn up from his satchel and slapped them onto the coffee table.

'I don't want to do a job for you, Caroline. I simply want you to sign the divorce papers and then never to clap eyes on you again.'

Her head rocked back, hurt gleamed in her eyes, and that soft, composed mouth of hers looked so suddenly vulnerable he hated himself for his outburst.

She rose, pressing her hands to her waist. 'That was unnecessarily rude.'

It had been.

She glanced at her watch. 'As interesting as this trip down memory lane has been, I'm afraid I'm going to have to ask you to leave. I have to be somewhere shortly.' She picked up the papers. 'I'll have my lawyer read over these and then we can get divorce proceedings underway.'

'And you'll draw the process out for as long as you can to punish me for refusing this job?' he drawled, rising too.

Her chin came up. 'I'll do nothing of the sort. You can have your divorce, Jack. The sooner the better as far as I'm concerned.'

A weight pressed down on him, trying to crush

his chest. It made no sense. She was promising him exactly what he wanted.

With an oath, he sat again.

Caro's eyes widened. 'What are you doing?'

'Finishing my coffee and cake. Sit, Caro.'

'Really, Jack! I—'

'It's hard, seeing you again.'

Her tirade halted before it could begin. She swallowed, her eyes throbbing with the same old confusion and hurt that burned through him.

The intensity of emotion this woman could still arouse disturbed him. It was as if all the hard work he'd put in over the last five years to forget her and get his life back on track could be shattered with nothing more than a word or a look. He couldn't let that happen. He straightened. He *wouldn't* let that happen.

'No woman has ever made me as happy as you did.' He sipped his coffee. 'Or as miserable. I wasn't expecting the lid to be lifted on all those old memories. It's made me…testy—and that's why I said what I said. It was a mean-spirited thing to say. I'm sorry.'

Finally she sat. 'It doesn't make it any less true, though.'

'It's not true. Not really.' He didn't look at her as he said it. 'I expect things will be more comfortable once we put this initial meeting behind us.'

'I expect you're right.'

She frowned suddenly and glanced a little to his left. With a swift movement she reached down and picked up... *His cufflinks!*

Jack bit back a curse. They must have fallen from his case when he'd pulled out the divorce papers. He could tell from the way her nostrils suddenly flared that she recognised the box. They'd been her wedding present to him when he'd said he'd prefer not to wear a ring—rose gold with a tiny sapphire in each that she'd claimed were nearly as blue as his eyes. He'd treasured them.

His glance went to her left hand and his gut clenched when he saw that she no longer wore her wedding ring.

Without a word she handed the box back to him. 'You really ought to be more careful when you're pulling things from your bag.'

He shoved the box back into the depths of the satchel. 'Tell me about this job you'd like me to do for you.'

He didn't owe her for her signature on their divorce papers, but if by doing this he could end things between them on a more pleasant note, then perhaps he'd find the closure he so desperately needed.

'And, yes, you have my word that I will never reveal to another soul what you're about to tell me—unless you give me leave to.'

She stared at him, as if trying to sum him up.

With a start he realised she was trying to decide whether to trust him or not.

'You don't trust my word of honour?'

'If you're after any kind of revenge on me, what I'm about to tell you will provide you with both the means and the method.'

He didn't want revenge. He'd never wanted revenge. He just wanted to move on with his life.

And to kiss her.

He stiffened. *Ridiculous!* He pushed that thought—and the associated images—firmly from his mind.

'I have no desire to hurt you, Caro. I hope your life is long and happy. Would it ease your mind if I didn't ask you to sign the divorce papers until after I've completed this job of yours?'

She leaned back, folding her arms. 'Why is this divorce so important to you now?'

'I want to remarry.'

She went deathly still. 'I see.'

She didn't. It wasn't as though he had a particular woman in mind, waiting in the wings, but he didn't correct the assumption she'd obviously made. It was beyond time that he severed this last tie with Caro. He should have done it before now, but he'd been busy establishing his company. Now it was thriving, he was a self-made success, and it was time to put the past to rest.

If Caro thought he'd fallen in love again, then all well and good. It would provide another layer of distance between them. And while he shouldn't need it—not after five years—he found himself clinging to every scrap of defence he could find.

'Well…' She crossed her legs. 'I wish you well, Jack.'

She even sounded as if she meant it. That shouldn't chafe at him.

'Tell me about this job you want to hire me for.'

He bit into the cake in an effort to ignore the turmoil rolling through him and looked across at her when she didn't speak. She glanced at the cake and then at him. It made him slow down and savour the taste of the sweet sponge, the smooth cream and the tiny crunch of sugar.

He frowned. 'This is really good.'

Finally she smiled. 'I know.'

He'd have laughed at her smugness, but his gut had clenched up too tightly at her smile.

She leaned forward, suddenly all business. 'I'm now a director at Vertu, the silver and decorative arts division at Richardson's.'

'Right.' He didn't let on that he knew that. When they'd married she'd been only a junior administrator at the auction house.

'Yesterday I placed into my father's safe a very beautiful and rather valuable snuffbox to show to a client this morning.'

'Is that usual?'

She raised one elegant shoulder. 'When selected

customers request a private viewing, Richardson's is always happy to oblige.'

'Right.'

'When I went to retrieve the snuffbox this morning it wasn't there.'

He set down his now clean plate, his every sense sharpening. 'You have my attention.'

'I put it in the safe myself, prior to the reading of my father's will.'

'Which took place where?'

'In my father's study—the same room as the safe.'

He remembered that study. He nodded. 'Go on.'

Her expression was composed, but she was twisting the thin gold bangle on her arm round and round—a sure sign of agitation.

'The fact that I am sole beneficiary came as a very great shock to both Barbara and I.'

He raised an eyebrow. 'Your father and Barbara have remained married all this time?'

'Yes. I believe she loved him.'

Jack wasn't so charitable, but he kept his mouth shut.

'When Barbara retired to her room, the lawyer gave me this letter from my father.' She rose, removed a letter from her purse and handed it to him. 'More cake?'

He shook his head and read the letter. Then he

folded it up again, tapping it against his knee. 'He thought she was stealing from him.'

Knowing Roland Fielding, he'd have kept a very tight rein on the purse strings. What kind of debts could his lovely young wife have accrued that would have her risking being caught red-handed with stolen goods?

'He was wrong. It wasn't Barbara who was pilfering those bits and pieces. It was Paul.'

'Paul is still working…?' He blew out a breath. 'Shouldn't he have retired by now?'

She pressed her hands together. 'My father wasn't a man who liked change.'

That was the understatement of the year.

'And, to be fair, I don't think Paul is either. I suspect the thought of retirement horrifies him.'

The bangle was pushed up her arm and twisted with such force he thought she'd hurt herself.

'He and Barbara have never warmed to each other.'

'And you're telling me this because…?'

'Because Paul was putting all those things he'd taken—'

'Stolen,' he corrected.

'He was putting them away for *me*.'

Jack pressed his fingers to his eyes.

'He was as convinced as I that I'd be totally written out of the will. He thought that I might need them.'

He pulled his hand away. 'Caro, I—'

She held up a hand and he found himself pulling to a halt.

'If Barbara finds out why my father wrote her out of the will and that Paul is responsible, she'll want him charged. I can't let that happen—surely you can see that, Jack? Paul was doing it for *me*.'

'You didn't ask him to!'

'That's beside the point. I know Barbara has been wronged, and I mean to make it up to her. I intend to split the estate with her fifty-fifty.'

He let the air whistle between his teeth. 'That's very generous. You could probably buy her silence for a couple of million.'

'It's not generous and I don't want to "buy her silence"! I want her to have half of everything. Half is certainly far more than I ever expected to get, and I'm fairly certain she won't begrudge me it.'

Was she?

'Where does the snuffbox come in?'

She hauled in a deep breath. 'During the middle of the night Barbara removed the jewellery from the safe. As it's all hers she had every right to remove it.'

He straightened. 'Except the snuffbox went missing at the same time?'

She nodded. 'When I asked her about it she claimed to not have seen it.'

'But you don't believe her?'

Her fingers started to twist that bangle again. 'She was upset yesterday—understandably. She wasn't thinking clearly. I know she wouldn't do anything to deliberately hurt me, but my father has treated her so very shabbily and I suspect she panicked. I fear she's painted herself into a corner and now doesn't know how to return the snuffbox while still maintaining face.'

'And you want me to recover said snuffbox without her being aware of it?'

'Yes, please.'

It should be a piece of cake. 'What happens if the snuffbox isn't restored to Richardson's?'

'I'll lose my job.' She let out a long, slow breath. 'I'll never work in the industry again.'

He suddenly saw what she meant by revenge. Her job had been more important to her than starting a family with him. Now he had the potential to help destroy all the credibility she'd worked so hard to gain in one fell swoop. The irony!

'Worse than that, though…'

He lifted a disbelieving eyebrow. 'Worse than you losing your job?'

Her gaze didn't waver. 'Richardson's prides itself on its honesty and transparency. If I don't return that snuffbox there will be a police investigation.'

'The scandal would be shocking,' he agreed.

'For heaven's sake, Jack—who cares about the scandal?' She shot to her feet, hands on hips. 'Barbara does *not* deserve to go to jail for this. And Paul doesn't deserve to get into trouble either.'

They were both thieves!

'This mess is of my father's making. He forces people into impossible situations and makes them desperate. I won't let that happen this time around. I won't!' She pulled in a breath and met his gaze squarely. 'I mean to make this right, Jack. Will you help me?'

He stared at her. This woman had dashed all his most tightly held dreams. Five years ago she'd ground them underfoot as if they hadn't mattered one iota. The remembered pain could still make him wake up in a lather of sweat in the middle of the night.

He opened his mouth.

His shoulders slumped.

'Yes.'

Since when had he ever been able to say no to this woman?

Caro tiptoed past the disused pantry, and the butler's and housekeeper's offices—both of which had been vacant for as long as she could remember. The kitchen stretched all along the other side of these old rooms, with the small sitting room Paul used as his office on the other side of the kitchen. She'd chosen this route so as to not disturb him, but she tiptoed just the same. The man had bat-like hearing.

Lifting the latch on the back door, she stepped out into the darkness of the garden, just as she'd promised Jack she would. She glanced around, wondering in what corner he lurked and watched her from. Feigning indifference, she lifted her head and gazed up at the night sky, but if there were any stars to be seen they were currently obscured by low cloud.

She knew from past experience, though, that one rarely saw stars here—the city lights kept the stars at bay and, as her father had always told her, star-gazing never got anybody anywhere in life.

'Tell that to astronomers and astronauts,' she murmured under her breath.

'Miss Caroline?'

Paul appeared in the kitchen doorway. Caro wiped suddenly damp palms down her skirt. No one was supposed to see her out here.

'Dinner will be ready in ten minutes.'

She turned towards him. 'Are you sure there isn't anything I can help you with?'

'Certainly not.'

In his youth, Paul had trained as a chef. With the help of an army of maids, who came in twice a week, Paul had kept this house running single-handed for nearly thirty years. Although, as her father had rarely entertained, the position hadn't been a demanding one.

When she was a child she'd spent most of the year away at boarding school. So for nearly fifteen years—before her father had married Barbara—it had just been her father and Paul rattling around together in this big old house.

Some sixth sense—a hyper-awareness that flashed an odd tingling warmth across her skin—informed her that Jack stood in the shadows of a large rhododendron bush to her left. It took all her strength not to turn towards it. She'd wanted to let Paul in on their plan—his help would have been invaluable, and for a start she wouldn't be tiptoeing through the house in the dark, unlatching doors—but Jack had sworn her to secrecy.

And as he happened to be the surveillance expert...

She reached Paul's side and drew him to the right, away from Jack, pointing up at the steepled roofline. 'Did you know that one night, when I was ten, I walked all the way along that roofline?'

Paul glanced up and pressed a hand to his chest. 'Good grief!'

'I'd read a book about a cat burglar who'd made his way across London by jumping from roof to roof.'

'Tell me you didn't?' Paul groaned.

She laughed. From the corner of her eye she saw

a shadow slip through the door. 'Mrs Thomas-Fraser's Alsatian dog started up such a racket that I hightailed it back to my room before the alarm could be raised.'

'You could've fallen! If I'd know about that back then it would have taken ten years off my life.'

Caro shook her head. 'I can hardly believe now that I ever dared such a thing. Seriously, Paul, who'd have children?'

He chuckled and patted her shoulder. 'You were a delight.'

To Paul, perhaps, but never to her father.

'Come along.' He drew her into the house. 'You'll catch a chill if you're not careful.'

She wanted to laugh. A *chill*? It was summer! He was such a fusspot.

'I don't suppose I could talk you into joining Barbara and I for dinner?'

'You suppose right. It wouldn't be seemly.'

Seriously—he belonged in an England of a bygone age. 'Oh, I should go and lock the other door.'

'I'll take care of it.'

To insist would raise his suspicions. 'Paul, do we have any headache tablets?'

He pointed to a cupboard.

When he'd gone, she popped two tablets and unlatched the kitchen door—just in case. This sneaking around business was not for the faint-hearted.

* * *

Barbara sliced into her fillet of sole. 'Caroline, do I need to remind you that if your father had *wanted* me to inherit any portion of his estate, he'd have named me in his will?'

Caro swallowed. 'You only call me Caroline when you're cross with me.'

Barbara's gaze lifted.

'I didn't know he was going to do this, Barbara. I swear. I wish he'd left it all to you.'

Her stepmother's gaze lowered. She fiddled with the napkin in her lap.

'And if he *had* left it all to you,' Caro continued, 'I know you'd have made sure that I received a portion of it.'

'Of course—but that's different.'

'How?'

'This money has been in your family for generations. It's your birthright.'

Twaddle. 'I mean to give Paul a generous legacy too. He'll need a pension to see him through retirement.'

'That man's a rogue. I wouldn't be surprised if he hasn't weaselled enough bonuses out of your father over the years to see him through *two* retirements.'

'Even if he has, he'll have earned every penny.'

The other woman's gaze narrowed. 'You and your father—you never could find any common ground. You didn't understand each other. You never brought out the best in him. And—you'll have to forgive me for saying this, Caro, darling—you were never at your best when you were around him either.'

Caro opened her mouth to dispute that, then shot her stepmother a half smile. How could Barbara still defend him after he'd treated her so shabbily? 'Okay, I'll concede that point.'

Where was Jack at this very moment? Was he in Barbara's room, scanning its every hiding place? Had he found the snuffbox yet?

The thought of Jack prowling about upstairs filled her with the oddest adrenaline rush—similar to the one she'd had as a ten-year-old, when she'd inched across the mansion's roof. It made her realise how boring her life had become.

Not boring! Predictable.

She stuck out her chin. She *liked* predictable.

'Caro?'

She snapped her attention back to Barbara.

'You had the oddest look on your face.'

Jack had *always* had that effect on her. 'Just trying to work out the morass that was my father's mind. *And* yours.'

'Mine?' Barbara set her fork down. 'Whatever do you mean?'

'If our situations were reversed you'd be happy

to share my father's money with me. Why aren't you happy for me to share it with you?'

Barbara picked up her clutch purse and rose. 'I find my appetite has quite fled. I really don't wish to discuss this any further.'

Caro nearly choked on her sole. *Jack!* If Barbara should happen to find him in her room…

'Please don't go! I—' She took a hasty sip of water. 'I'm tired of feeling lonely in this house.'

Barbara's face softened. She lowered herself back to her chair. 'Very well—but no more talk about your father and his money.'

'Deal.' Caro did her best to eat her new potatoes and green beans when all the while her stomach churned.

Please be careful, Jack.

She glanced over at her stepmother. 'Paul tells me you've barely been out of the house lately? Don't you think you should get out more? Being cooped up like this can't be good for you.'

Barbara sent her a tiny smile. 'On that subject we happen to be in complete agreement, darling. Lady Sedgewick has invited me down to their place in Kent this very weekend. She's having a house party. I thought I might accept her invitation.'

'Oh, yes, you should! The Sedgewicks are a lovely family. I was at school with Olivia. Do go. You'll have a lovely time.'

It was beyond time that Barbara started enjoying herself again.

Caro tiptoed into her room ninety minutes later. 'Jack?' she whispered into the darkness, before clicking on the light.

Her room was empty. She tried to crush the kernel of disappointment that lodged in her chest. He hadn't said that he'd wait for her in her room. She'd just assumed he would. She checked her phone for a text.

Nothing.

Maybe he'd sent her an email?

She was about to retrieve her laptop when a shadow on the far side of the wardrobe fluttered and Jack detached himself from the darkness. Her mouth went dry and her heart pounded. She tried to tell herself it was because he'd startled her, but she had a feeling her reaction was even more primal than fear.

Dressed in close-fitting jeans and a black turtleneck sweater, Jack looked dark, dangerous and disreputable.

Delicious, some part of her mind pronounced.

She wanted to tell herself to stop being ridiculous, but 'delicious' described him perfectly. What *was* ridiculous was the fact that every atom of her being should swell towards him now, with a hunger that robbed her of breath.

But why was it ridiculous—even after five years? It had always been this way between them.

Yes, but five years ago he'd broken her heart. *That* should make a difference.

She lifted her chin. It did. It made a huge difference. Obviously just not to her body's reaction, that was all.

She pulled in a breath. 'Well…?'

She held that breath as she waited for him to produce the snuffbox. She'd get her snuffbox and he'd get his divorce, and then he could marry this new woman of his and they'd all be happy.

He lifted a finger to his lips and cocked his head, as if listening to something.

Actually, she had serious doubts on the happiness aspect. She had serious doubts that Jack was in love.

Not your business.

Jack moved in close, leaned towards her, and for a moment she thought he meant to kiss her. Her heart surged to the left and then to the right, but he merely whispered in her ear.

'Go and check the corridor.'

His warm breath caressed her ear, making her recall the way he'd used to graze it gently with his teeth…and how it had driven her wild. The breath jammed in her chest. She turned her head a fraction, until their lips were so close their breaths mingled. She ached for him to kiss her. She ached to feel his arms about her, curving her body to his. She ached to move with him in a union that had always brought her bliss.

His lips twisted and a sardonic light burned in the backs of his eyes. 'Caro, I didn't come up here to play.'

His warm breath trailing across her lips made her nipples peak before the import of his words hit her. From somewhere she found the strength to step back, humiliation burning her cheeks.

'You should be so lucky,' she murmured, going to the door and checking the corridor outside, doing all she could to hide how rubbery her legs had become. 'All clear,' she said in a low voice, turning back and closing the door behind her. 'What did you hear?'

He merely shrugged. 'It's better to be safe than sorry.'

She did her best not to notice the breadth of his shoulders in that body-hugging turtleneck or the depth of his chest. 'Do you also have a balaclava?'

He pulled one from the waistband of his jeans.

She rolled her eyes and shook her head, as if having him here in her bedroom didn't faze her in the least.

'Did you get it?' She kept her voice low, even though Barbara's room was at the other end of the house and Paul's was another floor up, and he used the back stairs to get to it anyway. Nobody would be passing her door unless they'd come deliberately looking for her.

'No.'

'No?' She moved in closer to whisper, 'What do you mean, no?' She had to move away again fast—his familiar scent was threatening to overwhelm her.

'If it'd been in that room I would've found it.'

She didn't doubt him—not when he used that tone of voice. Damn! Damn! *Damn!*

She strode to the window, hands clenched. 'Where can it be?'

'Did she have a handbag or a purse with her at dinner?'

Caro swung around. 'A little clutch purse.' In hindsight, that *had* been odd. She hadn't had any plans to go out this evening, so why bring a purse to dinner in her own house?

'It's in there, then.'

'So…what now? You can't creep into her room with her in it.'

'It wouldn't be ideal,' he agreed, moving to the window and raising it. In one lithe movement he slid outside.

'So?'

'So now I go home and ponder for a while.'

She should have known it wouldn't be that easy. She planted her hands on her hips. 'Jack, you *can* use the front door. Everyone else is in bed. No one will see you.'

'But you've made me eager to try out your cat burglar method.'

So he'd heard her conversation with Paul about that…

She leaned out to peer at him. 'Be careful.'

He moved so quickly that she wouldn't have been able to retreat even if the gleam in his eyes *hadn't* held her captive. His lips brushed her hair, his breath tickling her ear again. She froze, heart pounding, as she waited for him to murmur some final instruction to her.

Instead his teeth grazed her ear, making her gasp and sparking her every nerve ending to life.

CHAPTER THREE

'I *KNEW* THAT was what you were remembering earlier. And your remembering made *me* remember.'

Jack's voice was so full of heat and desire it made Caro sway. 'So…' Her voice hitched. 'That's my fault too, is it?'

Jack, it seemed, considered everything to be her fault.

He ignored that to lean in closer again and inhale deeply. 'You smell as good as you ever did, Caro.'

She loathed herself for not being able to step away.

He glanced down at her and laughed—but it wasn't a pretty sound, full of anger and scorn as it was. She sensed, though, that the anger and scorn were directed as much at himself as they were at her.

He trailed a lazy finger along the vee of her blouse. Her skin goosepimpled and puckered, burning at his touch with a ferocity that made her knees wobble.

'If I had a mind to,' he murmured, 'I think I could convince you to invite me to stay.'

And the moment she did would he laugh at her and leave?

The old Jack would never have enjoyed humiliating her. And yet that finger continued trailing a tantalising path in the small vee of bare flesh at her throat. Heat gathered under her skin to burn fiercely at the centre of her.

She made herself swallow. 'If I had my heart set on you staying, Jack, you'd stay.'

That finger stopped. He gripped her chin, forcing her gaze to meet the cold light in his. 'Are you sure of that?'

She stared into those eyes and spoke with an honesty that frightened her. 'Utterly convinced.'

Air whistled between his teeth.

'You want me as much as you ever did,' she said. And, God help her, the knowledge made her stomach swoop and twirl.

'And you want me.' The words ground out of him from behind a tight jaw.

'But that wasn't enough the last time around,' she forced herself to say. 'And I see no evidence to the contrary that it'd be any different for us now either.'

She found herself abruptly released.

Jack straightened. 'Right—Barbara. Now I've had time to think.'

He'd *what*? All this time his mind had been working? It was all *she'd* been able to do to remain upright!

'If she's keeping that trinket so close then she obviously has plans for it.'

'Or is she looking for the first available opportunity to throw it into the Thames and get rid of incriminating evidence?'

He shook his head. 'Barbara is a woman with an eye on the main chance.'

She found herself itching to slap him. 'You don't even *know* her. You're wrong. She's—'

'I've come across women like her before.'

Did he class Caro as one of those women?

'And I'm the expert here. You've hired me to do a job and we'll do it my way—understand?'

She lifted her hands in surrender. 'Right. Fine.'

'Can you get us an invitation to this country party of Lady Sedgewick's?'

She blinked. 'You *heard* that?'

'I thoroughly searched Barbara's room and your father's study, as well as checking the safe.'

She stared at him. 'You opened the safe?'

He nodded.

'But you don't know the combination.'

He waved that away as if it were of no consequence. 'And on my way to the study I eavesdropped on what might prove to be a key piece of information. By the way, it's a nice touch to keep letting Barbara think you mean to give her half of the estate. Hopefully it'll prevent her from feeling too desperate and doing something stupid—like trying to sell something that doesn't belong to her.'

Caro's fingers dug into the window frame. 'It's *not* a ploy! I fully intend to give her half.'

'Lady Sedgewick?'

She blew out a breath and tried to rein in her temper. 'I can certainly ensure that *I* get an invitation.'

'And me?'

'On what pretext?' She folded her arms. '*Oh, and by the way, Lady S, my soon-to-be ex-husband is in town—may I bring him along?* That won't fly.'

He pursed his lips, his eyes suddenly unreadable. 'What if you told her we were attempting a reconciliation?'

A great lump of resistance rose through her.

'Think about it, Caro. Your snuffbox goes missing and then the very next weekend Barbara—who's apparently hardly left the house in months—makes plans to attend a country house party. Ten to one she has a prospective buyer lined up and is planning to do the deal this weekend.'

Hell, blast and damnation!

'This is becoming so much more complicated than it was supposed to.'

'If you don't like that plan there are two other strategies we can fall back on.'

She leaned towards him eagerly. 'And they are…?'

'We storm into Barbara's room now, seize her purse and take the snuffbox back by force.'

Her heart sank. Very slowly she shook her head. 'If we do that she'll hate me forever.'

'And that's a problem because…?'

'I know you won't understand, but she's *family*.'

He was silent for a moment. 'That was a low blow.'

His eyes had turned dark and his face had turned to stone. Her heart started to burn. 'I didn't mean that the way you've taken it.'

'No?'

Jack had grown up in Australia's foster care system. It hadn't been a brutal childhood, but from what she could tell it had been a lonely one.

She glanced down at her hand, shaking her head. 'But you won't believe me and I'm too tired to justify myself. Let's just say that confronting Barbara like that is a last-ditch plan.' Exhaustion stretched through her. 'Jack, shouldn't we be having this conversation inside?' Him falling off the roof would top off a truly terrible day.

'I'm perfectly comfortable where I am.'

Which was as far away from her and her world as he could get at this current moment. 'Fine. And this second alternative of yours?'

'You go to your employer in the morning and explain that the snuffbox is missing.'

And lose her job? Lose her professional reputation and the respect of everyone in her industry? Through no fault of her own? *No, thank you!* Besides, if the police investigation—and she had no doubt that there would be one—traced the snuffbox back to Barbara…

She shuddered and abruptly cut off that thought.

'I can see you're even less enthused about that option.'

She hated the tone of voice he used. She hated his irksome sense of superiority. She hated the opinion he had of her.

That last thought made her blink.

'So, will you get us an invitation to the Sedgewicks'?'

She gave a stiff nod. 'Yes.'

'Good girl.'

'Don't patronise me.'

'And it'll be best,' he continued, as if she hadn't spoken, 'if Barbara doesn't find out that we're planning to be there.'

'Hmm…awkward…'

He raised an eyebrow.

'But doable,' she mumbled. She folded her arms and glared at him. 'You *do* know we'll have to share a room at Lady Sedgewick's?'

Everyone would take it for granted that they were sleeping together.

He gave a low laugh. 'Afraid you won't be able to resist me, Caro?'

Yes! 'Don't be ridiculous.'

'Or are you afraid I won't be able to control myself?'

'If you can't,' she returned tartly, 'then I suggest you rethink your plans to remarry.'

'Never.'

A black pit opened up in her chest. The sooner Jack was out of her life for good, the better.

She flinched when he ran a finger down her cheek. 'Never fear, sweet pea. While your charms are many and manifold, they were *never* worth the price I paid.'

She flinched again at his words, and when she next looked up he was gone.

'Right. A weekend in the country. Very jolly.'

She closed the window and locked it. And then, for the first time ever, she drew the curtains.

'Was it difficult to swing the invitation?'

'Not at all.'

It was early Saturday morning and she was sitting beside Jack in his hired luxury saloon car. It all felt so right and normal she had to keep reminding herself that it was neither of those things. Far from it. She still didn't know how they were going to negotiate sharing a bedroom. She kept pushing the thought from her mind—there was no point endlessly worrying about it—but it kept popping back again.

'Tell me how you managed it.'

So she told him how on Thursday she'd 'just happened' to bump into her old schoolfriend Olivia Sedgewick at a place she knew Olivia favoured for lunch, and they'd ended up dining together.

The house party in Kent had come up in their idle chitchat, and Caro had confided her concerns that this would be Barbara's first social engagement since Roland had died. A bit later she'd mentioned meeting up with Jack again after all these years, and how the spark was still there but they were wanting to keep a low profile in London in case things didn't work out.

Of course things weren't going to work out.

'And…?' Jack prompted.

'Well, from there she came up with the brilliant plan of inviting us down for the weekend. We'll get a chance for some out-of-London couple time, with the added bonus that I can keep an eye on Barbara too.'

He laughed. 'You mean you deviously planted the idea in her mind and she ran with it!'

She shrugged. 'She's a lovely person. It wasn't hard.'

'It was masterfully done. I should hire you for my firm.'

He didn't mean it, but his praise washed over her with a warmth that made her settle back a little more snugly in her seat. 'I fear I'm not cut out for a life of subterfuge and undercover intrigue. I don't know how you manage it without getting an ulcer.'

His chuckle warmed her even more than his praise had.

'Barbara has no idea that we're coming?' he asked.

'None whatsoever. I told Olivia I didn't want Barbara thinking she was being a burden to me. I asked her if we could say that we'd met up only last night and she invited us down to her parents' for the weekend on the spur of the moment.'

'Excellent. I've had her tailed over the last few days, but there's nothing suspicious to report. It appears you've not had any suspicious visitors for the last couple of days either.'

'Oh, well…that's good.'

And at that point they ran out of conversation.

'I've…um…taken most of next week off as leave from work.' Just in case they had to do more sleuthing.

'Right.'

She itched to ask him about the woman he had back home in Australia—the one he planned to marry. How had they met? What was she like? Was she very beautiful? Did they set each other alight the way she and he once had? Or…?

She folded her arms. Or was this other woman simply a brood mare? A means to an end?

She couldn't ask any of that, of course. What Jack did with his life was no longer any concern of hers. It was none of her business.

She lifted her chin. 'We're having a glorious summer so far.' She gestured at the blue sky and the sunshine pouring in the windows.

At the same time he said, 'I take it you're not seeing anyone at the moment?'

She stiffened. None of *his* business. 'What does that have to do with anything?'

He sent her a sidelong glance, his lips twisting. 'Let's just say it could be awkward for all concerned if we happened to run into your current squeeze in Kent.'

She laughed. It was either that or cry. 'That would be terribly bad form indeed. We're safe, Jack. I have no current paramour.'

Unlike him.

For heaven's sake, let it go!

She shifted on her seat. 'You'd better fill me in on the plan.' She bit her lip. 'You *do* have a plan, don't you?'

'My plan is to watch and listen. I'm good at my job, Caro. And I'm very good at reading people.'

He'd been terrible at reading *her*.

'I can nose out a fishy situation at fifty paces.'

'Fine, but... What am *I* supposed to do?'

'Be your usual charming self.'

From anyone else that would have sounded like a compliment.

'Don't forget our cover story. We're supposed to be attempting a reconciliation.'

She had no hope of forgetting *that*.

'So the odd lingering look and a bit of hand-holding won't go astray.'

She swallowed, her mouth suddenly dry and her pulse suddenly wild. 'Absolutely.'

'And just be generally attentive.'

To him? Or to what was going on around them?

'Take your cues from me.'

Suddenly all she wanted to do was return to her tiny flat, crawl into bed and pull the covers over her head.

He sent her another sidelong glance and then reached out to squeeze her hand. 'Whenever you feel your resolve slipping think about the consequences of not getting that snuffbox back.'

Worst-case scenario? She'd lose her job with no hope of another and she'd be visiting Barbara in jail. She shuddered. No, no, *no*. She couldn't let that happen.

She squeezed his hand back. 'Excellent advice.'

'With the two of you, that brings our numbers up to a merry dozen,' said Cynthia—Lady Sedgewick—leading Caro and Jack into the drawing room, where she introduced them to several of the other guests. 'Olivia should be here any moment. Oh, and *look*, Barbie dear...' Cynthia cooed as Barbara walked in from the terrace. 'Did you know that Caro and Jack were joining us this weekend?'

Barbara pulled up short, her mouth dropping open.

'It was all very last-minute,' Caro said, going across to kiss her stepmother's cheek. 'I never had a chance to tell you.'

Jack moved across to shake Barbara's hand. 'Lovely to see you again, Barbara.'

For an awful moment, Caro had the oddest feeling that Barbara meant to snub Jack completely, but at the last moment she clasped his hand briefly before slipping her arm through Caro's and drawing her away.

'Why don't I help you to unpack? You can fill me in—' she glared over her shoulder at Jack '—on all the gossip.'

'I've put them in the room next to yours, Barbie.'

'I'll see that Caro's safely settled.' With that, Barbara led Caro out of the drawing room and up a rather grand staircase.

'Doesn't it set your teeth on edge, the way she calls you Barbie?' Caro asked in a low voice.

'It's just her way. More pressing at the moment

is the question of what you're doing here with Jack?'

'Ah…'

'No, no.' Barbara held up her free hand. 'Wait till we've gained the privacy of your room.'

So arm in arm they climbed the stairs in silence and walked along the grand gallery with all its family portraits until they reached the wing housing their bedrooms.

'Are you completely out of your mind?' Barbara demanded, the moment she'd closed the bedroom door behind them. 'That man broke your heart into a thousand little pieces and stamped all over it without so much as a by-your-leave. Have you taken leave of your senses?'

Caro opened her mouth. Closing it again, she slumped down to the blanket box sitting at the end of the bed—which, thankfully, wasn't some huge big four-poster monstrosity.

'How long?' Barbara asked.

She and Jack should have discussed their cover story in a little more detail. She decided to go with the truth. 'Only a few days. I…I didn't know how to tell you.'

'A few *days*! And already you're spending the weekend with him?'

Caro grimaced at how that sounded. 'Well, technically we *are* still married. And I thought coming down here this weekend would…would…' She trailed off, wishing this all felt as make-believe as it actually was.

Barbara sat beside her and reached out to halt the constant twisting of her bangle. 'Caro, darling, I know your father's death came as a very great shock to you, but do you *really* think this is the best way to deal with it?'

'You think I'm making a mistake?'

'Don't you?'

Her shoulders sagged. 'You're probably right. Why are we so attracted to the things that are bad for us?'

Barbara opened her mouth and then closed it, her shoulders sagging too. 'It's a very strange thing,' she agreed.

'Seriously, though,' Caro said, strangely close to tears, 'what hope does a woman like me have of holding the attention of a man like Jack?'

Barbara stiffened. 'Don't you *dare* sell yourself short! Any man would be lucky to have you.'

Her stepmother's concern warmed her to her very bones. Surely Barbara wouldn't steal from her? She'd just got herself into a fix and she didn't know how to extricate herself. That was all.

She met Barbara's gaze. 'You really do care about me, don't you?'

'Of course I do. What on earth would have you thinking otherwise?'

'Father.'

'Look, darling, the will—'

'Not the will. I meant before that. All Father's disapproval and disappointment where I was concerned.' She lifted a shoulder and then let it drop. 'You must've resented all the...disharmony I caused.'

Barbara patted Caro's hand. 'I was married to your father, and I loved him, but it doesn't follow that we agreed on every point.'

She stared at the other woman, wondering what on earth that meant.

'And now Jack's back in your life...'

Not for long.

'And you think the spark is still there?'

She huffed out a breath. 'No doubt about that...'

Barbara went to Caro's suitcase and flung it open, rummaged through its contents. 'Here.' She pulled out a pair of tight white Capri pants and a fitted blouse in vivid blue. 'Slip into these. They'll be perfect for croquet on the lawn later.'

Caro grimaced. 'There's nowhere to hide in that outfit.' She normally wore a long tunic top with those Capris. 'And there's no denying I've put on a little weight in the last few months.'

'Despite what torture we women put ourselves through in the name of beauty, men appreciate a few curves on a woman. Jack won't be able to take his eyes off you.'

Barbara smiled at her and Caro found herself

smiling back. Dressing to attract Jack suddenly seemed like the best idea in the world.

And fun.

Besides, *he* was the one who had insisted on their ridiculous cover story. She was only doing what he'd insisted was necessary. No harm in enjoying herself in the process...

Jack watched Caro ready herself to take her next shot and had to run a finger around the collar of his shirt when she gave that cute little tush of hers an extra wiggle. He wasn't the only man admiring her...uh...feminine attributes. His hand tightened about his croquet mallet. It was all he could do not to frogmarch her up to the house and order her to put on something less revealing.

Except what she was wearing was perfectly respectable! The only bare flesh on display was from mid-calf to ankle, where her Capris ended and her sand shoes started. Those sand shoes made her look seriously cute. The only problem was they kept drawing his attention to the tantalising curves of her calves.

Who was he trying to kid? Her entire ensemble made her look cute. Not to mention desirable.

Barbara trailed over to him, a glass of fruit punch dangling elegantly from her fingers. 'Caro is looking well, isn't she?'

He couldn't lie. 'She's looking sensational.' But then he'd *always* thought she looked sensational.

Some things never change.

Barbara smiled up at him pleasantly. 'May I give you a word of warning, darling?'

'Of course.'

'If you break her heart again, I will cut *your* heart out with a knife.'

Whoa!

With a bright smile, she patted his arm. 'Enjoy your game.'

He stared after her as she ambled off again.

'You're up, Jack.'

He spun around to see Caro pointing to the hoop that was his next target. Croquet? He scowled. What a stupid game!

'Cooper!' Caro called to one of the other players. 'Have you added any new pieces to your collection recently?'

Good girl.

'Dear me, yes. I picked up a rather splendid medieval knife at the quaintest little antique place.'

Don't tell Barbara that. It might give her ideas.

'I must show it to you next time you're over.'

How well did Caro know these people?

He took his shot and tried to focus as the conversation turned to collectibles and antiques. He entirely lost the thread of it, though, when Caro took her next shot. Did she *practise* that maddening little shimmy?

He glanced around, gritting his teeth at the appreciative smiles on the other men's faces. He couldn't frogmarch her up to their bedroom and demand she change her clothes! If he marched her up to their bedroom he'd divest her of those clothes as quickly as possible and make love to her with a slow, serious intent that would leave her in no doubt how much he, for one, appreciated her physical attributes.

Every cell in his body screamed at him to do it.

He ground his teeth together. He was here to do a job. He was here to put the past behind him. It had taken too long to get this woman out of his system. He wasn't letting her back into his life again. Regardless of how cute her tush happened to be.

Find the snuffbox.

Get the divorce papers signed.

Get on with your life.

He kept that checklist firmly in the forefront of his mind as he turned his attention back to the conversation.

Croquet was followed by lunch. After lunch it was tennis and volleyball. A few of the guests went riding, but as Barbara was lounging in a chair on the lawn, alternately chatting with their hostess and flicking through a glossy magazine, he and Caro stuck close to the house too. Besides, Jack didn't ride.

It suddenly struck him that he had no idea whether Caro rode or not. Just another of the many things that hadn't come up during their short marriage.

Caro smiled a lot, chatted pleasantly and seemed utterly at ease, but it slowly and irrevocably dawned on him that while she'd always been somewhat reserved and self-contained that was even more the case now. She seemed to hold herself aloof in a way she never had before. She'd become more remote, serious…almost staid.

Dinner was followed by billiards for some, cards for others and lazy conversation over drinks for the rest. The other guests were a pleasant lot, and despite his low expectations he'd found it an oddly pleasant day.

Except for the lingering glances Caro sent him. And the secret smiles that made him want to smile back…and then ravish her. He'd lost count of the number of touches she'd bestowed on him—her hand resting lightly on his arm, her fingers brushing the back of his hand, her arm slipping through his…

Goddamn endless touches!

He raised his hand to knock on their shared bedroom door, but then pulled it back to his side.

He had to get a grip. Caro was only following his instructions. Even if she *was* in danger of over-doing it.

Overdoing it? Really?

He ground his teeth together. No. She'd struck the perfect balance. He just hadn't realised that her flirting with him would stretch the limits of his control so thoroughly.

Be cool. Keep a lid on it.

Hauling in a breath, he knocked. He'd given her a good thirty minutes to get ready for bed. He hoped it was enough. It would be great if she were asleep.

The door opened a crack and Caro's face appeared. *No such luck.* She moistened her lips and opened the door wider to let him enter. She wore a pair of yoga pants and an oversized T-shirt…and her nerves were plain to see in the way she was pushing her bangle up and down her arm. It sent an answering jolt through him and a quickening of his pulse. If she'd had access to some of his earlier thoughts she'd have every right to her nerves.

He resisted the urge to run his finger around his collar again. He had to get his mind off the fact that they were in a bedroom. Alone.

He draped his jacket across the back of a chair. 'I've been meaning to ask—has Barbara ever exhibited any signs of violence?'

Caro settled on the end of the bed, her feet

tucked up beneath her. 'Heavens no. Why would you ask such a thing?'

He raked both hands back through his hair, trying not to look at her fully. 'During croquet she threatened to cut my heart out with a knife if I broke *your* heart.'

'Ah.' She bit her lip and ducked her head. 'So that's what put you off your game.'

He could have sworn her shoulders shook. He settled himself in the chair—the only chair in the room. It was large and, as he'd be spending the night in it, thankfully comfortable.

'Are you laughing at me?'

'Not *at* you.' Her eyes danced. 'But she's such a tiny little thing, and you have to admit the thought of her doing you any damage is rather amusing.' A smile spilled from her. 'And it's kind of sweet for her to fluff up all mother-hen-like on my account.'

That smile. He had a forbidden image of her sprawled across that bed, naked...wearing nothing but that smile.

A scowl moved through him.

She shrugged. 'It's nice.'

Nice? He stared at her, and for the first time it occurred to him that extracting Barbara from this mess—one of her own making, he might add—might, in fact, be more important to Caro than her job. Which was crazy. He'd had firsthand experience of all Caro would sacrifice in the interests of her career.

'That's why she whisked me away the moment we arrived. She wanted to warn me of you—to tell me to be careful.'

He stared at her. 'Careful of what?'

'Of *you*, of course. Of getting my heart broken again.'

'*Your* heart?' He found himself suddenly on his feet, roaring at her. 'What about *my* heart?'

Her jaw dropped. '*Your* heart? *You* were the one who walked away without so much as a backward glance!' She shot to her feet too, hands on hips. 'You mean to tell me you *have* a heart?'

More than she'd ever know.

He fell back into the chair.

She folded her arms and glared. 'Besides, *your* heart can't be in any danger. You're in love with another woman, right?'

He moistened his lips and refused to answer that question. 'Are you saying *your* heart is in danger?'

She stilled before hitching her chin up higher. 'When you left five years ago I thought I would die.'

He wanted to call her a liar. Her heart was as cold as ice. It was why he'd left. He hadn't been able to make so much as a dent in that hard heart of hers. But truth shone from her eyes now in silent accusation, and something in his chest lurched.

'I am *never* giving you the chance to do that to me again.'

For a moment it felt as if the ground beneath his feet were slipping. He shook himself back to reality.

'Sending me on a guilt trip is a nice little ploy, Caro, but it won't work. I *know* you, remember?'

'Oh, whatever...' She waved an arm through the air, as if none of it mattered any more, and for some reason the action enraged him.

He shot to his feet again. She'd started to lower herself back to the bed, but now she straightened and held her ground.

'You!' He thrust a finger at her nose. 'You made it more than clear that while I might be suitable rebellion material, to put Daddy's nose out of joint, I was nowhere near good enough to father your children!'

That knowledge, and the fact that she'd taken him in so easily, should have humiliated him. He wished to God that it had. He wished to God that he'd been able to feel anything beyond the black morass of devastation that had crushed him beneath its weight.

All he'd ever wanted was to build a family with this woman. A family that he could love, protect and cherish.

Before Caro, he hadn't known it was possible to love another person so utterly and completely. When he'd found out that she didn't love him back, he hadn't known which way to turn.

One thing had been clear, though. He'd had no intention of leaving her. He'd blamed her father, with all his guilt-tripping emotional blackmail, for stunting Caro's emotional development. He'd figured that half or even a quarter of Caro was worth more than the whole of any other woman.

That was how far he'd fallen.

She'd stamped all over him—and he'd spread himself at her feet and let her do it.

When he'd asked her if they could start a family, though, she'd laughed. *Laughed.*

He dragged a hand down his face. He would never forget the expression on her face. He hadn't been able to hide from the truth any longer—Caro would never consent to have a family with him.

So he'd left before he could lose himself completely.

He'd fled while there was still something of him left.

'*Your* heart?' he spat. 'What use did *you* ever have for a heart? Stop playing the injured party. You haven't earned the right.'

CHAPTER FOUR

'I HAVEN'T EARNED the right…?'

Caro's hands clenched and she started to shake with the force of her anger. He watched with a kind of detached fascination. Back when they'd been married—*they were still married*—Caro had rarely lost her temper.

In fact, now that he thought about it, she might have got cross every now and again, but he couldn't recall her *ever* losing her temper. To see her literally shaking with anger now was a novel experience…and bizarrely compulsive.

Her eyes flashed and a red flush washed through her cheeks. She looked splendid, alive—and tempting beyond measure. There was nothing staid or remote about her now.

He loathed himself for the impulse to goad her further.

He loathed himself more for the stronger impulse to pull her into his arms and soothe her.

He watched her try to swallow her anger.

'In your eyes, my not wanting children made me unnatural. Having children was more important to you than it ever was for me. It's a very great shame we didn't discuss our views on whether or not we wanted children *before* we married.'

He stabbed a finger at her. 'What's a *very great shame* is that your job—your stupid, precious job—was more important to you than me, our relationship and the potential family we could've had.'

The old frustration rose up through him with all its associated pain.

'What's so important about your job? What is it, after all, other than vacuous and frivolous? It can hardly be called vital and important!'

Her eyes spat fire. 'What—unlike *yours*, you mean?'

He swung away and raked a hand through his hair, trying to lasso his anger before swinging back to face her. 'When you get right down to it, what do you *do*? You sell trinkets to rich people who have more time and money than they do sense.'

Her hands clenched so hard her knuckles turned white. 'While *you* find things rich people have lost? Oh, that's *right* up there with saving lives and spreading peace and harmony throughout all the land.'

He blinked as that barb found its mark. 'My job's saving your butt!'

'Not yet it isn't!'

They stared at each other, both breathing hard.

'If people like me didn't care about our jobs, Mr High and Mighty, *you'd* be out of work.'

Touché.

'Sometimes jobs aren't about performing an important function in society. Sometimes they're about what they represent to the people doing them.' She thumped a hand to her chest, her voice low and controlled. '*My* job is the only thing I've ever achieved on my own merit. Against my father's wishes, strictures and censure *I* chose the subjects *I* wanted to study at university.'

She'd chosen Art History rather than the Trust Law and Business Management degree her father had demanded she take. He'd wanted her groomed in preparation for taking over that damn trust he'd set up in her mother's name. Caro had always sworn she wouldn't administer that trust, but her father had refused to believe her, unable to countenance the possibility of such rebellion and defiance.

'*My* job,' Caro continued, 'has provided me with the means to pay the rent on my own flat and to live my own life. How dare you belittle that? My job has given me independence and freedom and the means—'

'I understand you needing independence from your father.' Fury rose through him. 'But you didn't need it from *me*! I'm nothing like your father.'

'You're *exactly* like my father!'

She'd shouted at him, with such force he found himself falling back a step. His mouth went dry. She was wrong. He was nothing like her father.

'You wanted to control me the same way he did. What *I* wanted didn't matter one jot. It was always what *you* wanted that mattered!' Her voice rose even higher and louder. 'You didn't want a wife! You wanted a…a *brood mare*!'

The accusation shot out of her like grapeshot and he stared at her, utterly speechless. He couldn't have been more surprised if she'd held a forty-five calibre submachine gun complete with magazine, pistol grip and detachable buttstock to his head and said, *Stick 'em up.*

He found himself breathing hard. She was kidding—just trying to send him on a guilt trip. That couldn't be how she'd felt all those years ago.

The bedroom door flew open and they both swung round to find Barbara standing in the doorway, her face pinched and her eyes wide. 'I will *not* let you shout at Caro like that!'

Him? Caro had been the one doing most of the shouting.

'Come along, darling, you can bunk in with me tonight.'

She moved past Jack to take Caro's arm and tug her towards the door. She shot a venomous glare at him over her shoulder.

Caro didn't look at him at all. Not once. His heart started to throb. He opened his mouth to beg her to stay.

To what end? It was madness even to consider it. He snapped his mouth shut, clenching his hands into fists.

'Oh, *really*, Caro...' He heard Barbara sigh before the door closed behind them. '*This* is what you wear to bed to attract a man? It won't do.'

He wanted to yell after them that there was absolutely nothing wrong with what Caro was wearing, that she looked as delectable as ever. But, again, to what end?

He collapsed back into the chair, his temples throbbing and his chest burning.

'You wanted a brood mare!'

Behind her calm, composed facade, was that what she'd really been thinking? He rested his head in his hands. Was that truly how she'd felt? Was it how *he'd* made her feel?

'Are you okay, darling?'

Caro managed a shaky smile. 'This will probably sound stupid, but that's the very first time I've ever yelled at Jack.'

Barbara lowered herself to the bed. 'Coming

from anyone else I would be surprised—shocked, even—but not from you. You've always been a funny little thing.'

'Funny?'

'Very controlled and self-contained. You have a tendency to avoid confrontation. It can be very difficult to get a handle on how you truly feel.'

Caro blinked and sat too. 'I'm sorry. I didn't realise.'

'Oh, I know you don't do it on purpose. Besides, you're getting better.'

She rubbed a hand across her forehead. 'Fighting like that doesn't feel *better*.'

'So things with you and Jack aren't going so well?'

She recalled, despite their fight, that she and Jack had a cover story to maintain. She forced a shrug. 'That fight has been brewing for five years.'

'Well, then, maybe it's cleared the air,' Barbara said briskly. 'In the meantime, it won't hurt him to stew for a night. Now, come along—jump into bed. Things will look brighter in the morning, after a good night's sleep.'

'Are you sure you don't mind me sharing with you?'

'Not in the slightest.'

Caro climbed under the covers. Just before the light clicked out she noticed Barbara's clutch purse, sitting on the dressing table on the other side of the room like an unclaimed jackpot.

She blinked, her mind growing suddenly sharp. With a heart that pounded she lay still, staring into the dark, willing Barbara to fall asleep. The sooner she retrieved the snuffbox, the sooner Jack would be out of her life.

It seemed an age before Barbara's slow, steady breaths informed Caro that she was asleep. As quietly and smoothly as she could, she slid out from beneath the covers and stood by the side of the bed for a couple of moments, holding her breath to see if Barbara would stir.

When she didn't, she made her way carefully around the bed to the dressing table. Reaching out a hand to its edge, she nearly knocked over the can of hairspray sitting just behind the purse. With a dry mouth she righted it and waited. When nothing happened, she edged her fingers forward until they skimmed across the purse.

With her heart pounding so loudly she was sure Barbara must hear it, she opened the purse and pushed her hand inside. At the same moment the bedside light was flicked on.

'Caro, what are you doing?'

Caro stared into the clutch purse, afraid that if she turned around her expression would betray her. *No snuffbox.* 'I was…I was looking for some painkillers.' She turned and blinked in what she hoped was a bleary fashion.

'Here you go.' Barbara handed her a pill from a bottle on the bedside table beside her, along with a glass of water.

There was nothing for it but to take the head-ache tablet, even though she didn't have a head-ache. Granted, Jack was a major headache, but she'd need something stronger than an aspirin to get rid of *him*.

'Thank you, and I'm sorry I disturbed you.'

She climbed back into bed, her stomach feeling suddenly odd. Seriously, she wasn't cut out for all this sneaking around.

She wondered if Jack was sleeping soundly next door. She wondered what would have happened if she'd stayed there. Would they have made wild, abandoned love?

She tingled all over at the thought.

Just as well she was on this side of the wall!

The fuzziness of sleep settled over her, but when Barbara slipped from the bed Caro tried to push it away. What was Barbara doing? This could be a *clue*!

The other woman padded over to the window. Caro tried to rouse herself from the darkness try-ing to claim her.

As if from a long way away, she thought she

heard Barbara say, 'Oh, Roland, why did you have to make things so hard?'

Caro wouldn't mind an answer to that question herself. She tried to lift herself up onto her elbows, but her body refused to comply with the demand.

'Why are you making me do this?'

Do what?

Caro opened her mouth to ask, but the words wouldn't come. Her last coherent thought before a thick, suffocating blanket descended over her was that Barbara hadn't given her an aspirin. She'd given her a sleeping tablet.

Caro found it nearly impossible to shrug the fog of sleep from her brain, but she did manage to push herself upright into a sitting position.

What time was it?

Sunlight flooded in at the window, but finding the energy to locate a clock in this unfamiliar room seemed beyond her at that moment. She turned her head a fraction to check the bed. No Barbara. At least not in the bed.

'Barbara?'

She barely recognised that voice as her own.

She cleared her throat and tried again. 'Barbara?'

The result wasn't much better. Eventually she forced herself to sit on the edge of bed, and then to stand and turn around. It only confirmed what she already knew—Barbara wasn't in the room.

She hoped Jack knew where Barbara was.

She pulled in a breath. *Right*. She needed to go next door and dress and then join everyone else for the day's activities.

She made swaying progress across to the door. She had to rest for a moment before opening it, forcing herself through it and then closing it behind her. She'd almost reached the door to the room she and Jack shared when his voice sounded behind her.

'Caro?'

She rested back against the wall—needing its support—before turning her head in his direction. *Heavens*. A sigh rose up through her. With his height and his breadth, Jack cut a fine figure. A pair of designer denim jeans outlined his long lean legs and strong thighs to perfection. She'd bet the view looked even better from behind.

It suddenly occurred to her that if he'd come in a few minutes later he'd have almost certainly caught her in a state of undress. For some reason she found that almost unutterably funny, and a giggle burst from her.

'Morning, Jack.'

His eyes narrowed as he drew nearer. 'Have you been drinking?'

'Most certainly not.' She tried to straighten, but

only lasted a couple of seconds before she found herself slumping again. She pointed a finger at him. 'Barbara gave me a pill last night.'

His face darkened. 'You accepted a pill from Barbara? Are you *insane*?'

She didn't like his opinion of Barbara, and she *hated* his opinion of her. 'I thought it was an aspirin. And I had to take it to maintain my reason for why she'd caught me with my hand in her purse.' She frowned. 'I think it was a sleeping tablet... I'm still feeling kind of fuzzy.'

His nostrils flared, and he made a move as if to pick her up, but she held up both hands to ward him off.

'Ooh, please don't do that. My stomach is feeling... um...queasy. A bathroom would be a very good idea about now.'

He took her arm with a gentleness that had the backs of her eyes prickling. 'Come on—it's just a couple of doors this way.'

She tried not to focus on his strength, his warmth, or how much she was enjoying the feel of him beside her. It was this physical craving for him that had been her undoing before. It was something that went beyond sex. It had brought her peace and a sense of belonging that she'd felt right down in her very bones.

And it had obviously been a lie. So she needed to ignore it now.

'Where's Barbara?'

'She and a couple of the other women have gone into the village. Apparently there's a little boutique Cynthia has been gushing about.'

'Then why are you here?'

'I have an operative tailing them.'

She stopped and blinked up at him. 'You have *operatives*?'

His lips twitched. 'I have several, and this one is female. Believe me, she'll blend in much better than I ever could on a shopping trip.' He gestured to the door where they'd stopped. 'Do you need a hand?'

'Certainly not.'

'Then you have to promise me to not lock the door.'

'Will *you* promise not to come in?'

He crossed his heart. 'Unless you call me.'

'Deal.'

She wasn't sick, although it felt like a close run thing for a minute or two. Splashing cold water on her face had helped. So did the glass of water Jack pressed on her once they reached their room again.

He fluffed up the pillows and then helped her onto the bed to sit up against them. It made her feel oddly cared for.

'I'm sorry to be such a bother,' she mumbled. 'I've never had a sleeping tablet before.' She wouldn't have had one last night either if she'd known what it was.

'They don't agree with everyone.' He touched the backs of his fingers to her forehead. 'But your colour is returning and you don't feel hot.'

Don't focus on his touch! 'That's good, right?'

One side of his mouth hooked up. 'That's good.'

Don't focus on his smile! 'The snuffbox wasn't in Barbara's purse.'

He eased away from her, all businesslike and professional again, and she tried to tell herself that she was pleased about that.

'I'm going to go and check her room.'

'What? *Now?*'

'No time like the present.'

She swallowed and called out, 'Be careful.'

But as he was practically out of the room by the time she'd uttered the caution, he probably didn't hear it.

Sitting there, with her pulse racing too hard and her ears primed for Barbara's return, was even more nerve-racking than the night he'd searched the house in Mayfair.

She wondered why he was doing this when he didn't have to. She'd made it clear that she'd sign the divorce papers whether he helped her or not.

Because he wanted closure?

She rested her head back against the pillows. Things had grown so complicated between them five years ago. It occurred to her now that she hadn't moved on from then—last night's argument had proved that. She'd only pretended to. And this morning proved that she needed to stop craving that sense of belonging she'd only ever felt with him. She had to put that behind her too.

It was time to stop feeling like half a person. It was time to get on with her life.

And there was only one way to achieve that.

The door opened and Jack moved back inside. She raised an eyebrow.

He shook his head. 'Nothing.'

'I'm starting to think she's telling the truth—that she didn't take it.' She frowned. 'Except…'

He sat in the chair on the other side of the room. 'Except…?'

'Before I fell asleep last night, I heard her talking to my father.'

He raised an eyebrow.

'Not a hallucination—give me some credit, Jack. She was staring out of the window, talking to the dead like we all probably do from time to time.'

'Speak for yourself.' He shuffled forward an inch. 'What did she say?'

'She asked my father why he'd made things so hard, and…' She frowned trying to remember more clearly. 'And something about why was he making her do this…or something along those lines.'

'Your father left you *everything*?'

'Everything.'

'Without a single condition?'

'Condition-free.'

He shook his head and settled back in the chair. 'I could've sworn he'd make the management of your mother's trust a condition of the will.'

'I told him not to bother—that I refused to be dictated to that way.'

'And he believed you?'

She almost laughed. 'He ought to have done. I told him often enough. Why?'

'Just trying to get a handle on why he did what he did.'

She'd given up on that. It was an impossible task.

She and Jack both fell quiet. Her heart started to pound. She recalled Barbara's words from last night—about the way Caro was controlled and self-contained, and how she avoided confrontation. Five years ago she'd thought Jack had *known* how much she loved him. Maybe he hadn't. Maybe she hadn't been demonstrative enough.

'I'm going to talk about the elephant in the room,' she announced, her mouth going dry.

'What elephant?'

'The termination I had five years ago.'

Every muscle in his body bunched, as if she'd just hit him and he was waiting to see if the blow would fell him. Her heart burned so hard it made it difficult to continue. Except she had to continue. If Jack knew the truth maybe he wouldn't hate her so badly—maybe he wouldn't carry such a great weight of bitterness around with him. And…and maybe he'd find happiness with this new woman he had in his life.

The thought reduced her heart to ashes.

She moistened her lips, ignoring the blackness welling inside her. 'I spent hours and hours in those first weeks after you'd gone trying to work out why you'd left the way you had.'

She'd returned from work one evening to find every trace of him removed from their shared flat and a note informing her that he'd realised they wanted different things and he was returning to Australia. He'd left her no contact number, no way for her to get in touch with him. It had taken her months before she'd finally believed that he was never going to ring.

'And did you come to any conclusions?'

Oh, his bitterness! How could it still score her heart so deeply?

'Of course I did. I do have a fully functioning brain in my head.' Her voice came out too tart, but she couldn't help it. 'I decided that you must've somehow found out about the termination I was planning to have.'

He gave one terse nod. 'The clinic rang to confirm your appointment.'

'They *told* you?' That shocked her. They'd assured her of confidentiality.

'No, Caro, they didn't. But I'm a detective, remember? It didn't take much for me to put two and two together.'

'And yet you still only came up with three and three-quarters of the answer.'

He didn't yell, he didn't storm around the room flinging out his arms and accusing her of killing their child, but the way he stared at her with throbbing eyes didn't feel much better.

He tilted up his chin. 'I understand your right to make your own decisions when it comes to your body. I don't dispute that. But to get rid of a child I so desperately wanted...' He turned grey. 'That was when I realised you'd *never* have children with me.'

The children that had always been more important to him than she'd ever been.

'That was when I realised you'd meant it when you said you didn't want children.'

'I said I wasn't *ready* for children.'

There was a difference. Why had he never been able to understand that? She'd asked him to give her three years. Not that she'd been able to promise him for certain that they'd have children after that time either, but she'd needed time to consider the issue, to make sure in her own mind that she was up to the task of being a mother.

The thought of becoming a parent in the image of her father had filled her with horror. Jack's idea of family hadn't helped much either—it had seemed more like a fantasy she'd never be able to bring off. The whole issue of creating a family had left her all at sea, and it had been too big a decision to get wrong.

'Caro—'

'Jack, my pregnancy was ectopic.'

He froze. If silence could boom, it boomed now.

'Do you know what that means?' she ventured.

'Yes.'

She barely recognised the voice that croaked from his throat. She wanted to cover her eyes at the expression of self-disgust that spread across his features, millimetre by slow millimetre.

'It means the fertilised egg implanted itself in your tubes rather than in your uterus.'

She nodded and swallowed. 'In an ectopic pregnancy the foetus has no chance of surviving.'

'And if the foetus isn't removed it will kill the mother.' Her surprise at his knowledge must have shown, because he added, 'I had a foster mother who had an ectopic pregnancy.' He lifted his head. 'You had no choice but to have a termination.'

'No,' she agreed.

He shot to his feet, his body shaking and his eyes blazing. 'Why the *hell* didn't you tell me?'

'I was trying to find a way, but you left before I could! Why didn't you confront me about it as soon as you took that call from the clinic?'

He paced the room, a hand pressed to his forehead.

Caro pushed her bangle high up onto her arm, where the thin metal cut into her. She loosened it and tried to get her breathing back under control. 'I was trying to find the courage to face your disappointment,' she said.

He swung back to stare at her.

'To tell you I was pregnant in one breath and then to take it away in the next...' She shook her head. It had seemed unnecessarily cruel. 'It brought my most frightening fears to the surface. I couldn't help wondering if, down the track, it ever came to a question of my life or a baby's—which would you choose?'

He fell down into the chair.

'When you walked away I had my answer.'

Jack stared at Caro, his heart feeling as if it had been put through a grater and then the pieces collected up and shoved back into his chest willynilly. Had he ever really known her?

He'd walked away from his marriage believing

Caro had betrayed him and his dreams…and in the end it was he who'd betrayed *her*.

'You should've told me.' He didn't yell the words this time, but they shook with the force of emotion ripping through him.

'And *still* you blame me.'

Her remote smile troubled him. 'No!' His hands clenched. 'I'm just as much to blame. I can't believe I walked away over such a stupid misunderstanding.'

'That misunderstanding wasn't *stupid*, Jack. And with the benefit of hindsight it wasn't unforeseen either. Maybe you *should* blame me—because God knows I was glad the decision had been taken out of my hands. I was glad I wasn't faced with the choice of working out what to do with an unexpected pregnancy.'

It didn't change the fact that he'd walked away from her at a time when she'd needed his support.

'I'm sorry you had to go through that alone.'

She blinked, and her surprise at his apology hurt.

She moistened her lips. 'Thank you.'

He rubbed the back of his neck, silently calling himself every dark name he could think of.

'Was the procedure…gruelling?'

She shook her head. 'It was very simple keyhole surgery. The procedure was performed in the morning and I was home again in the afternoon.'

But he hadn't been there to cosset her afterwards.

She lifted a hand to push her hair off her face. Her hand shook and his heart clutched.

'I had a couple of stitches in my belly button and—' She swallowed. 'It didn't seem like much to show for...for all that was lost.'

Her words ran him through like a knife. He had to brace his hands on his knees to fight the nausea rising through him.

'I'm sorry I wasn't there for you. I'm sorry I left like I did.'

She glanced away, but not before he'd seen the tears swimming in her eyes.

In two strides he was in front of her and pulling her into his arms. She pressed her face into his shoulder and sobbed silently for a few seconds.

'When I first found out I was pregnant, there was a part of me that was excited.' One small hand beat against his chest. 'For a few moments I thought I could make everything work.'

His eyes and throat burned. She wrenched herself out of his arms and he felt more bereft than ever.

She seized a handkerchief from the nightstand and dabbed her eyes. 'You want to know something funny? If I ever *do* decide I want children I now have less chance of conceiving.'

His head rocked back. 'That's not funny! It's—'

'You leaving like you did…' She swung around. 'Maybe it was for the best after all.'

Did she really believe that?

She lifted her chin. 'What you said in your letter was true. We did want different things. We probably still want different things. You still obviously want children.'

His heart thumped.

She lifted a hand and let it drop. 'Me…? Even after all this time I'm still not certain I do. That would never have worked for you in the long run, Jack.'

In five years his desire for a family had never waned. If anything, it had grown. And in his pursuit of that he'd hurt this woman badly.

'I know it's a moot point now, but I wonder if you'd have married me if you'd known I couldn't have children.'

He stared at her and shook his head. 'I can't answer that. I haven't a clue.'

And now they'd never know.

He pulled in a breath. One thing was clear—this time he wasn't leaving until the job was done and he and Caro had said everything they needed to say.

Five years ago he'd misjudged her and her actions. He'd make that up to her, and then maybe he'd be able to draw a line under this part of his life and move on. Without bitterness and without blame.

CHAPTER FIVE

'WHAT DO YOU MEAN, you believe Barbara drugged me on purpose? You really are set against her, aren't you?'

Jack kept his eyes on the road, but his every sense was attuned to the woman sitting next to him in the car. She smelt like caramel, and with every agitated movement she sent another burst of sweetness floating across to him.

It would take less than seventy-five minutes to reach Mayfair from the Sedgewick country estate, but he had no faith in his ability to last the distance with that scent tormenting him.

'She wanted nothing more than to comfort me after the fight you and I had, and to make sure I got a decent night's sleep.'

'She wanted to make sure you didn't find the snuffbox.'

His hands clenched about the steering wheel. He'd put Caro in danger. He'd underestimated Barbara's desperation and the lengths she'd go to in an effort to not get caught. His jaw tightened. What if Caro had reacted adversely to the sleeping pill? What if—?

'Barbara *cares* about me.'

His knuckles turned white. 'Barbara is determined to save her own skin! Why can't you see this issue in black and white for once, instead of a hundred shades of grey?'

The words burst from him more loudly than he'd intended and they reverberated through the car with a force that made her flinch. He cursed himself silently.

Except... 'You need to be on your guard around her, Caro. You need to tread carefully where she's concerned.'

He glanced across and her deep brown eyes momentarily met his. The confusion in them made his chest ache. Her gaze lowered to his hands and his white-knuckled grip on the steering wheel. He tried to relax his fingers. He wanted her on her guard—not frightened witless.

'Regardless of what you think, this issue is *not* black and white.'

He had to bite his tongue. This had always been a bugbear between them. She'd always claimed he was too quick to make snap judgments. He'd retaliate by saying she lacked judgment.

'I think she has a lover,' he bit out.

Barbara had buried her husband three months

ago—a husband she claimed to have loved. If she had taken up with another man so soon after Roland's death it wouldn't add credibility to her claims of devotion.

Caro straightened and swung towards him. It was all he could do to keep his eyes on the road and his hands on the wheel.

'What makes you think that?' she asked.

'She bought lingerie on her shopping trip to the village this morning.'

To his chagrin, she started to laugh. 'Heaven forbid that a woman should buy pretty undergarments for her own pleasure.'

'In my experience—'

'*Your* experience?' She folded her arms. 'Exactly how many lovers have you had in the last five years, Jack?'

His head rocked back, the question barrelling into him and knocking him off balance. No doubt as it had been intended to.

His heart thudded. 'You first.' The savagery that ripped through him made his stomach churn. 'If you really want to know the answer to that, then you answer first.'

Spots appeared at the edges of his vision while he held his breath and waited for her to answer. That was what the thought of Caro with another man did to him. Even after five years.

'It's none of my business,' she said after a long pause. 'I'm sorry.'

At her apology, it was as if a hand reached out and squeezed his chest in a grip that stole his breath. One moment he wanted to rip her apart and the next he wanted to draw her into his arms and never let her go. It made no sense whatsoever.

'It doesn't feel that way, though, does it?' he growled. 'Our *business* still feels intertwined.'

'I know.' Her chest rose and fell in a sigh. 'Which is ludicrous after all this time.'

He swallowed the ball of hardness doing its best to lodge in his throat. 'It could be because our relationship had no formal ending.' He'd just…*left*. 'There were no last words, no proper goodbyes.'

'Perhaps,' she agreed, her voice full of dejection and…and secrets?

'One,' he snapped out.

'I beg your pardon?'

He didn't need to turn his head to imagine in technicolour detail the slow blink of her eyes and the cute wrinkle of confusion that would appear between her eyebrows.

'In the last five years—since I left you—I've had one lover, Caro.'

One. He didn't turn his head. He didn't want to see the surprise that would be plastered across her face.

She coughed. 'One? *You—one?*'

He almost smiled then, because he knew that in about five seconds she'd be internally beating herself up for revealing her surprise, her shock. She'd deem it rude and insensitive.

'One,' he repeated.

'But…' Her hands made agitated movements in the air. 'But you like sex so *much*!'

He'd loved it with Caro.

'So do you.'

He couldn't continue this conversation and keep driving at the same time.

On impulse he turned in at a small pub. 'Hungry?' At a stretch they could make this an early dinner.

'Not in the slightest.' She unbuckled her seatbelt and opened her door. 'But a glass of burgundy would go down a treat.'

They sat at a table by the far wall, nursing their drinks.

'And I can hardly call her a lover,' Jack said.

Caro shot back in her seat, one hand pressed to her chest just above her heart, drawing his attention to the pale perfection of her throat.

'Please, Jack, you don't have to explain. You don't owe me anything.'

Yes, he did.

'It was a one-night stand,' he continued, 'and it was a disaster.'

The entire time the only person he'd been able

to think about had been Caro. It had been Caro's touch he'd craved, and he'd used another woman in an attempt to drive Caro from his mind. Not only hadn't it worked, it had been unfair. The encounter had left him feeling soiled, dirty and ashamed. He hadn't been eager to repeat the experience.

Caro brought her wine to her lips and sipped. Her hand shook as she placed the glass back to the table. 'It's only been the once for me too. I wanted to get on with my life. I wanted to feel normal again.'

He could tell it hadn't worked.

'It was terrible. It left me thinking I should join a convent.'

He grimaced.

She stilled. He glanced across at her. She twisted her bangle round and round with sudden vigour.

'What?' he demanded.

'You don't have a woman waiting back home for you in Australia, do you?'

He glanced away.

'You want to remarry, and you still want children…' She let out a breath. 'But you don't have anyone specific in mind yet.'

Something inside him hardened. 'Why are you so relieved about that?'

'Because I *knew* you weren't in love. I thought you were about to make another mistake.'

He stared at her, at a loss for something to say.

'You want to feel normal again too. That's what all this is about.'

He thrust out his jaw. 'It's time to draw a line under us.'

She stared down into her red wine, twirling the glass around and around instead of her bangle. 'So…we're working towards—what? An amicable divorce?'

Acid burned in his stomach. He took a sip of his beer in an attempt to ease it. 'And getting your snuffbox back.' He owed her that much.

She suddenly straightened, and although she leaned towards him he couldn't help feeling she'd erected some emotional barrier between them.

'Barbara doesn't have a lover, Jack. She bought that lingerie for *me*. I'm afraid she doesn't subscribe to the view that yoga pants and a T-shirt are suitable attire for the bedroom. She thinks I should be making more of an effort to attract you.'

A groan rose up through him.

'So, in case you need to know this in support of our cover story, it's a long gold negligee with shoestring straps and some pretty beading just here.'

Her hands fluttered about her chest and it took an effort of will for him not to close his eyes. 'Right…'

Her eyes grew sharp. 'And yet you still think she could hurt me?'

He straightened too. 'Why don't you just throw her to the wolves?' The woman was a thief, for God's sake!

'I care about her. She…she and Paul…are like family to me.'

She said the word *family* carefully, as if afraid it might hurt him.

He gulped back a generous slug of beer. 'Some family!'

She sipped her red wine, but her jaw was tight. 'You *do* know your idea of family is too romantic, don't you?'

That was what happened when you grew up without one of your own.

Her eyes narrowed, as if she'd read that thought in his face.

'I hope you find what you're looking for, Jack. I really do. I hope it makes you as happy as you seem to think it will.'

He sensed her sincerity. And her doubt. 'Not all families are as screwed up as yours, Caro.'

'That's very true. But Barbara…' She shrugged. 'I feel a certain affinity with her. My father turned her into a trophy wife, never correcting the widely held view that people had of her. Probably because he found the depth of his feelings for her too confronting. So he tried to control her…and she let him. Unlike me, she did everything he asked of her—everything she could to please him. And if you think that was easy then you're crazy.'

He could feel his mouth gape. He snapped it shut. 'You're *nothing* like Barbara.'

'That's where you're wrong. All I'd have had to do was agree to have children with you, Jack, and I'd have been exactly like her.'

'That was totally different!'

'How?'

'I *never* tried to turn you into a trophy wife.'

'No—just into the mother of your children.'

He ground his teeth together. 'Asking you if we could start a family was not an unreasonable demand.'

'My father didn't see ordering me to take over the administration of my mother's trust as an unreasonable demand either. He thought it a worthy goal. And he was right—it is. But it's not a role I want in life.'

In the same way, she obviously didn't want the role of mother.

'For God's sake, Caro, I *loved* you!'

'But not unconditionally! It was clear you'd only continue to love me if I bore your children.'

His hand clenched about his glass. 'What you're saying is that what you wanted was more important than what *I* wanted.'

She lifted her glass, but she didn't drink from it.

'I don't recall you ever offering to be the primary caregiver. I don't recall you ever making any attempt at compromise.'

Each word was like a bullet from a Colt 45.

'I was the one who was expected to make all the sacrifices.'

Bull's eye. For a moment Jack could barely breathe.

'But that's all old ground.' She waved a hand in the air and sipped her wine. 'Do you seriously think Barbara could present a physical danger to me?'

It took an effort of will to find his voice…his balance…his wits. 'I'm not ruling it out.'

'Then let's call the search off.'

She drained the last of her wine and he found it impossible to read anything beyond the assumed serenity of her countenance.

'For God's sake, why?'

'I don't want to force her into actions she'd otherwise avoid. If she's as desperate as you're implying, then she's welcome to the snuffbox.'

'But your job…?'

'I'll have to explain that I've lost the snuffbox, make financial reparation to the seller, and then tender my resignation.'

She'd sacrifice her *job*? She *loved* her job.

'I could go back to university.'

'To study what?'

'Something different from my undergraduate degree, obviously. Or I could enrol in a doctorate programme. It's not like money will be an issue.'

But there'd be a cloud hanging over her head, professionally, for the rest of her working life. Regardless of their differences and their history, she didn't deserve to take the blame for someone else's wrongdoing. Caro was innocent and he was determined to prove it.

'No!'

She raised an eyebrow and rose casually to her feet, though he sensed the careful control she exerted over her movements.

'I believe we're done here.'

He rose too. 'Give me until the end of the week, Caro. Like we planned. Give me until Friday. It's only five days away.'

She opened her mouth and he could see she was going to refuse him.

'Please?'

His vehemence surprised her, but he couldn't help it.

'I swear I won't put Barbara in any position that will incite her to violence.'

She glanced away and then glanced back. Finally she nodded. 'Okay—but then it's done, Jack. It's finished.'

He knew what she really meant, though. They'd be done. Finished.

The resistance that rose through him made no sense.

He nodded, and then took her arm and led her out to the car. 'Am I taking you back to the house in Mayfair or to your flat?'

'The flat, please.'

Good. He didn't want to run into her when he bugged the Mayfair house tonight…

Caro frowned at the knock on her door. She dumped her notepad on the sofa before seizing the remote and clicking the television off.

Daytime television, Caro? How low do you mean to sink?

Shaking her head, she padded to the door and opened it.

'Hello, Caro.'

Jack!

She moistened suddenly dry lips, wishing she'd bothered to put on something more glamorous than the default yoga pants when she'd dragged herself out of bed this morning.

'Uh, good morning?'

She started and glanced at her watch, huffed out a sigh. 'Yep, it's still morning.'

'Just.'

Right.

'May I come in?'

She blinked, realising she'd been holding the

door open and just staring at him. 'Of course. I'm afraid I wasn't expecting to see you today.'

He entered without saying a word. He sported those same designer jeans he'd worn yesterday and the view from the back was indeed spectacular. It wasn't his physique that held her attention, though—as drool-inducing as those shoulders and butt might be—but the odd combination of stiffness and stillness in his posture that hinted at… nervousness? What did Jack have to be nervous about?

Oh, dear Lord! Unless he had news for her. *Bad* news.

She pushed her shoulders back, forced her chin up. She'd already decided the snuffbox was lost forever, hadn't she? She'd accepted the fact that she'd lose her job. She pulled in a breath.

'You've found out something? You have…bad news?'

He shook his head. 'I'm currently collecting information and analysing data.'

No, he wasn't. He was here in her flat. Her *tiny* flat.

Widening his stance, he eyed her up and down. Warmth crept across her skin and a pulse fired to life deep inside her. Soon, if she weren't careful, he'd have her throbbing and pulsing with the need he'd always been able to raise in her.

She crossed her arms, not caring how defensive

it made her look. Once upon a time she'd have sashayed over to him, run her hands along his shoulders and reached up on tiptoe to kiss him—long, slow, sensuous kisses that would have had him groaning and hauling her close...

She clenched her hands. But that had been back before he'd left. That had been before he'd broken something inside her that she hadn't been able to put back together. She wasn't kissing Jack again and they most certainly weren't going to make love together. It would set her back five years!

She stared back at him. She didn't know if there was a challenge in her eyes or not, but the hint of a smile had touched his lips.

'I'm afraid Barbara wouldn't approve.'

It took a moment for her to realise he referred to her yoga pants and T-shirt. 'Barbara never drops around unannounced.'

He took neither the bait nor the hint, just nodded and glanced around her sitting room. For once she wished it were larger, not quite so cosy. His gaze zeroed in on the plate of cake perched on the coffee table. He turned back and raised both eyebrows.

Her cheeks started to burn. Dear Lord! She'd been caught sitting around in her slouchy pyjamas, eating cake and watching daytime television. What a cliché!

She refused to let her humiliation show. 'I'm on

leave this week. It's a well-known fact that when one is on holiday, cake for breakfast is mandatory.'

He didn't point out that it was nearer to lunch-time than breakfast.

'Besides, that orange cake is utterly divine—to die for. Would you like a slice?'

He shook his head.

She pulled in a breath, counted to three and then let it out. 'I really wasn't expecting to see you today, Jack. I don't mean to be rude, but what are you doing here?'

His eyes shone bluer than she remembered. They seemed to see right inside her—but that had to be a trick of the light.

'I was hoping to take you to lunch.'

Her heart gave a funny little skip. 'Why?'

'There are some things we should discuss.'

Divorce things? She didn't want to talk about the divorce. Why couldn't they just leave it up to their lawyers? She wanted to say no to lunch. She wanted to say no to spending more time in his company. She wanted to resist the appeal in those eyes of his. Those eyes, though, had always held a siren's fascination for her.

'Is it really such a difficult decision?'

To admit so would be far too revealing, but to go to lunch with him...

'I just don't see the point.'

'Does there need to be a point? It's a beautiful day outside.'

Was it? She glanced towards the window.

'And maybe I'm striving for the *amicable* in our amicable divorce.'

Was she supposed to applaud him for that?

In the next moment she bit her lip. Was he worried that she'd become difficult and spiteful if he didn't recover the snuffbox?

She frowned. Surely not? Surely he knew her better than that...

Her heart started to pound. Very slowly she shook her head, recalling the expression on his face when she'd revealed the true reason behind her medical termination. His shock had swiftly turned to self-disgust and guilt. She didn't want him racked with guilt. She was just as much to blame as him for that particular misapprehension. Besides, that one incident hadn't been responsible for the breakdown of their marriage. It had just been the proverbial last straw.

'Caro?'

She raised her hands in surrender. 'Fine. I'll go and get changed.'

Twenty minutes later they were outside, walking in the sunshine. Jack was right—it was a glorious day.

She lifted her face to the sun and closed her

eyes. 'I love this time of year. I wish it could be summer all year long.'

'Which begs the question, why were you cooped up in your flat when you could've been outside, enjoying all of this?'

'Maybe because my leave is for a family matter rather than a true holiday? Maybe because I don't actually feel in a holiday mood?'

'So the cake…?'

'Cake is its own reward,' she averred stoutly, trying to resist the way his chuckle warmed her to her very toes.

They were quiet until they reached the Thames. Caro turned in the direction of several riverside cafes and restaurants. The river was dark, fast-flowing and full of traffic. She loved its vibrancy… the way it remained the same and yet was always changing.

'When did you stop having fun, Caro?'

Her stomach knotted. 'I beg your pardon?' She slammed to a halt, planting her hands on her hips. 'I have fun!'

How dare he try to make her life all black and white with his judgments?

The dark seriousness in his eyes made her heart beat harder. 'I'll have you know that I have plenty of fun! Oodles of it! I catch up with my girlfriends regularly for coffee.' *And cake.* 'I see shows, go to movies, visit art galleries. I live in a city that offers a variety of endless activities. I have plenty of fun, thank you!'

'You've had nothing in your diary for the last three months.'

She clenched her hands to stop from doing something seriously unladylike. 'You went through my diary?'

'It was on the coffee table…open. I figured if it were sacrosanct you'd have put it away.'

'Or maybe I expected better manners from my visitors!' Heat scorched her cheeks. 'That is one of the rudest things I've ever heard. An invasion of privacy and—'

'Not as rude as stealing a snuffbox.'

She folded her arms and with a loud, 'Hmph!' set off again at brisk pace. 'You were looking for clues?'

'Just wondering if you'd made any enemies lately.'

She rolled her eyes, wondering why it was so hard to rein in her temper. 'I'm not the kind of woman to make enemies, Jack.'

Except of her father.

And her husband.

'Is there anyone at Richardson's who's been fired recently? Someone who might hold you responsible? Is there some guy who's been pestering you for a date over the last three months? Have you had a disgruntled client who's cross they've missed out on a particular treasure? Is there—?'

'No!'

'Caro, your diary is full of work commitments, the odd work-related lecture at London University or an art gallery, and one weekend conference in Barcelona. You didn't have a single dinner date, coffee date, movie date, *any kind of date* scheduled into your diary at all.'

'Maybe because it's a *work* diary. I remember my social engagements. I don't need to write them down.'

It struck her now that there were so few invitations these days they were easy to remember. She went cold and then hot. When had that happened? She'd once had a full calendar.

'You always were a good liar.'

He said it as if it were a compliment!

'I'm sorry to say, though, that I don't believe you.'

'And that should matter to me because…?'

He flashed her a grin that set her teeth on edge. 'Getting under your skin, aren't I, kiddo?'

'Don't call me that!' It had been a pet name once. Jack had drawled it in Humphrey Bogart fashion and it had always made her smile.

Not any more.

'You were only ever that rude when you were fibbing or hiding something.'

'And it seems you can still try the patience of a saint.'

God knew she wasn't a saint. But his perception had her grabbing hold of her temper again, and her composure, and trying to twitch both into place.

'You wrote *everything* down. You were afraid you'd forget otherwise. You were big on making lists too.'

'People change. Believe it or not, in the last five years even *I've* changed.'

'Not that much.' He pulled a folded sheet of paper from his pocket. 'You still make lists.'

She snatched it from him, unfolded it and started to shake. 'This… You…'

'That's a list you're making of options in the eventuality of losing your job.'

'I know what it is!' She scrunched the sheet of paper into a ball. 'You had no right.'

'Maybe not, but it brings us back to the original question. When did you stop having fun, Caro?'

Before she could answer, he marched her to a table for two at a nearby riverside restaurant and held a chair out for her. For a moment she was tempted to walk away. But that would reveal just how deeply he'd got under her skin, and she was pig-headed enough—just—not to want to give him that satisfaction.

Besides—she glanced around—the sun, the river and the warmth were all glorious, and something deep inside her yearned towards it. She didn't want to turn her back on the day—not yet. For the first time her flat suddenly seemed too small, too cramped.

Blowing out a breath, she sat. For the briefest of moments Jack clasped her shoulders from behind in a warm caress that made her chest ache and her stomach flutter.

He took the seat opposite. 'Caro—'

'Pot.' She pointed to him. 'Kettle.' She pointed to herself. 'When was the last time *you* had fun?'

The waitress chose that moment to bustle up with menus.

Manners, Caro.

'They do a really lovely seafood linguine here.' The Jack of five years ago had loved seafood. She figured he probably still did.

'Oh, I'm sorry,' the waitress said, 'but that's no longer on the menu. We've had a change of chef.'

Jack glanced at Caro and then leaned back in his chair. 'When did you change chefs?'

'It'd be four months ago now, sir.'

Caro swallowed, staring at the menu without really seeing it. 'My…how time flies.'

Jack said nothing. He didn't have to. Had it really been over four months since she'd been down here for a meal?

They ordered the prawn and chorizo gnocchi that the waitress recommended, along with bottles of sparkling mineral water. When the waitress moved away, Caro hoped that Jack would drop the subject of fun. She hoped she could simply...

What? Enjoy a pleasant lunch in the sunshine with her soon-to-be ex-husband? That didn't seem likely, did it?

She gestured to the river, about to make a comment about how fascinating it always was down here, watching the river traffic, but she halted at the expression on his face.

'You're not going to let the subject drop, are you?'

'Nope.'

'Why does it matter to you one way or another if I have fun or not?'

'Because I can't help feeling that I'm to blame for the fact you don't have fun any more—that it's my fault.'

He couldn't have shocked her more if he'd slapped her.

She folded her arms on the table and leaned towards him. 'Jack, I get a great deal of enjoyment out of many things—a good book, a good movie, cake, my work—but I think it's fair to say that I'm not exactly a pleasure-seeker or a barrel of laughs. I never have been.'

'You used to make me laugh. Now, though, seems to me you hardly ever laugh.'

'Has it occurred to you that it's the company I'm currently keeping?'

He didn't flinch—not that she'd said it to hurt him—but his gaze drifted out towards the river and she couldn't help feeling she'd hurt him anyway.

Their food arrived, but neither one of them reached for their cutlery. She touched the back of his hand. His warmth made her fingertips tingle.

'I didn't say that to be mean, but neither one of us should pretend things are the same as they used to be between us—that things aren't…difficult.'

She went to move her hand, but in the blink of an eye he'd trapped it within his. 'When was the last time your soul soared, Caro? When was the last time you felt like you were flying?'

Her mouth dried. She wasn't answering that.

The last time had been on a picnic with Jack in Hyde Park. They'd packed a modest meal of sandwiches, raspberries and a bottle of wine, but everything about that day had been perfect—the weather, the world…them. They'd gone home in the evening and made love. They'd eaten chocolate biscuits and ice cream for dinner while playing Scrabble. That day had felt like perfect happiness.

Had that day been worth the pain that followed?

She shook her head. She didn't think so.

He released her hand. 'I see.'

Did he?

'Just as I thought.'

She forced a morsel of food into her mouth. 'The gnocchi is very good.'

'I bought a boat.'

She lowered her cutlery with a frown. *Okaaay.*

'I go boating and fishing. And some days when I'm standing at the wheel of my boat, when I'm whipping along the water at a great rate of knots and the breeze is in my face, sea spray is flying and the sun is shining, I feel at peace with the world. I feel alive.'

He lived near water? 'What made you get a boat?'

'A couple of friends, tired of my…grumpiness, dragged me out on their boat.'

Her jaw dropped. 'Grumpiness?' Caro felt like an idiot the minute the word left her. She tried to cover up her surprise by adding, 'You obviously enjoyed it enough to buy your own boat.'

'When I left you and returned to Australia I threw myself into work.'

He'd made such a success of his firm that only an idiot could accuse him of wasting his time.

'But I didn't do anything else—just worked. I didn't want to be around people. I just wanted to be left alone.'

She could relate to that.

'Apparently, though, being a bear of a boss isn't the ideal scenario.'

Ah...

'A couple of friends dragged me out on their boat, where I was quite literally a captive audience, and proceeded to tell me a few home truths.'

She winced. 'Ouch.'

'They pointed out that I had no balance in my life.'

'So you bought a boat?'

He shrugged. 'It helped.'

'I'm glad, Jack, I really am. But…' She leaned back, her stomach churning. 'Why are you telling me this?'

'Because I want to help you find *your* boat.'

CHAPTER SIX

HE WANTED TO help her rediscover her passion, but she was suddenly and terribly afraid that they'd simply discover—*re*discover—that *he* was her passion. What would they do then?

You could offer to have a family with him.

No! She didn't want to live with a man who placed conditions on his love. She'd had enough of that growing up with her father. Why couldn't *she* be enough?

Oh, stop whining!

Jack stared at her, as if waiting for her to say something, but she was saved from having to answer when a little girl moved close to their table, her face crumpling up as is she were about to cry.

Caro reached out and touched the little girl's shoulder. 'Hello, sweetie, have you lost your mummy?'

The little girl nodded, her eyes swelling with tears.

'Well, I'll admit that's frightfully easy to do,' Caro continued in her usual voice—she hated the way adults put on fake voices where children were concerned, 'but shall I let you into a secret?'

The child nodded.

'Mummies are very good at finding their little girls.'

'You think Mummy will find me?'

'Oh, yes, I know she will.'

Caro was aware of Jack's gaze—the heaviness in it, the heat…his shock.

'The trick, though, is to just stay put and wait.' She glanced at the food on the table. 'Would you like a piece of garlic bread while you wait? My friend here—' she gestured to Jack '—thought I was hungry and ordered a lot of food, but…' She started to laugh. 'I had cake for breakfast, so I'm not really hungry at all.'

The little girl's eyes went wide. 'You ate *cake* for breakfast?'

'Uh-huh.'

'Is it your birthday?'

'Nope—it's just one of the good things about being a grown-up.'

In no time at all the little girl—Amy—was perched on Caro's lap, munching a piece of garlic bread. Caro didn't want to meet Jack's eyes, so she looked to the left of him, and then to his right.

'You might want to keep an eye out for a frantic-looking woman.'

'Right.'

She turned her attention back to the little girl. It was easier to look at her than at the yearning she knew would be stretching through Jack's eyes.

The sight of Caro holding that little girl, her absolute ease with the child, burned through Jack. A dark throb pulsed through him. They could have had this—him and Caro. They could have had a little girl to love and care for. If only Caro hadn't been afraid.

If only I'd been patient.

The thought slid into him, making his heart pound. She'd asked him for time but he'd thought she was putting him off, making excuses. So he hadn't given her time. In hindsight he hadn't given her much of anything.

Unable to deal with his thoughts, he stood and scanned the crowd, doing as Caro had suggested and trying to locate a worried mother in the crowd. It took less than a minute for a likely candidate to appear. He waved to get the woman's attention, and in no time flat—with a multitude of grateful thank-yous—the pair were reunited.

He sat.

Caro reached for her mineral water. 'Stop looking at me like that.'

'Like what?'

'Just because I don't know if I want children of my own it doesn't mean I don't like them.'

'Right…'

She glared at him then, before skewering a prawn on the end of her fork. For some reason, though, *he* was the one who felt skewered.

'Why on earth did you—*do* you,' she amended, 'want children so much?'

He shrugged, but his chest tightened, clenching in a cramp, and for a moment he couldn't speak.

Eventually he leant back. 'I've always wanted children…for as long as I can remember.'

'Well, now, *there's* a strong argument to convince a woman to change her entire life to fit children into it.'

With that sally, she popped the prawn into her mouth and set to picking through what was left of her pasta, obviously in search of more prawns.

A scowl built through him. 'Can't a person just want kids?'

She shrugged. 'Maybe. My next question, though, would be… Do you want children because you believe you can give them a good life and help them to grow up to be useful members of society? Or…?'

'Or…?'

'Or do you want children because you've never had a proper family of your own, have always felt lonely, and feel that children will fill that lack in your life?'

He stared at her, breathing hard. 'That's a mean-spirited thing to do, Caro—to use my background against me.'

Her forehead crinkled. 'I'm not trying to use it against you. I'm truly sorry you had such a difficult childhood. I sincerely wish that hadn't been the case. But at the same time I don't believe children should be used to fill gaps in people's lives. That's not what children are meant for.'

'Why didn't you ask me any of this five years ago?'

She set her fork to the side. 'I doubt I could've verbalised it five years ago. Your craving for children made me uneasy, but I could never pinpoint why.'

Jack wanted to get up and walk away—which, it appeared, was his default position where this woman was concerned.

'And, you see,' she continued, staring down at her plate rather than at him, 'back then it played into all of my insecurities.'

Her what?

'And that made me withdraw into myself. I realise now I should've tried to talk to you about this more, but I felt that in your eyes I wasn't measuring up.'

Her words punched through him. 'Just as you feel you never measured up in your father's eyes?' He let out a breath, seeing it a little more clearly now. 'If I'd had a little more wisdom… But your withdrawal fed into all of *my* insecurities.'

Her forehead crinkled in that adorable way again. *Don't notice.*

'Insecurities? *You*, Jack? Back then I thought you the most confident man I'd ever met.'

When he'd been sure of her love he'd felt like the most invincible man on earth.

'I saw your refusal to have children with me as a sign that I…' He pulled in a breath and then forced the words out. 'That I wasn't good enough for you to have children with.' He dragged a hand back through his hair. 'I thought that as a brash colonial from the wrong side of the tracks I was only good enough to marry so you could thumb your nose at Daddy…'

She straightened. 'I'll have you know that I've never thumbed my nose at anyone in my *life*!'

'I thought I wasn't the right *pedigree* for you.'

Her shoulders slumped. 'Oh, Jack, I was never a snob.'

He nodded. 'I can see that now.'

Her shoulders slumped further. 'I'm sorry you felt that way. If I'd known…'

'If you'd known you'd have set me straight. Just like I'd have set *you* straight if I'd known I was making you feel like *you* weren't measuring up.'

She pulled in a breath and lifted her chin. 'It's pointless wallowing in regrets. We live and learn.

We'll know better than to make the same mistakes in the future...with the people who come into our lives.'

He understood what she was telling him. That there was no future for them regardless of whatever acknowledgments and apologies they made for the past now.

Beneath the collar of his shirt his skin prickled. Of *course* the two of them had no future. She didn't need to remind him!

She pushed away from the table a little. 'It's been a lovely lunch, Jack, but—'

'We were talking about boats.'

She rolled her eyes. 'I don't need a boat. I don't *want* a boat.'

'When did you become so risk-averse? *Everyone* needs a boat, Caro—a figurative one—even you. You had passions once.'

Her cheeks flushed a warm pink. His skin tightened. He hadn't been referring to that kind of passion, but he couldn't deny that as lovers they'd had that kind of passion in spades. The one place where they hadn't had any problems had been in the bedroom. She'd been everything he'd ever dreamed of...and everything he hadn't known to dream of.

He wanted her now with the same fierceness and intensity with which he'd wanted her five years ago. The way her eyes glittered told him she wanted him too. They could go back to her flat and spend the afternoon making wild, passionate love. That would help her rediscover her passion for life.

For how long, though? Until he left and returned to Australia?

A knot tightened in his stomach. They couldn't do it. It would only make matters worse.

Caro glanced away and he knew that regardless of how much he might want it to, she'd never let it happen.

Which was just as well. His hands clenched. This time when he left he wanted to leave her better off than when he'd found her. They might still want different things out of life, but that didn't mean he couldn't help her rediscover her joy again.

He set his shoulders. 'You said you'd give me to the end of the week.'

'To find my snuffbox!'

'We need people to believe we're reuniting… we don't want them suspecting that I'm working for you.'

That was a lowdown dirty trick, but he could see that it had worked.

She folded her arms and glared at him. 'To the end of the week,' she growled.

He had to hook his right ankle around his chair-leg in order to remain seated rather than shoot to his feet, reach across the table and kiss her.

The fingers of her right hand drummed against her left arm. 'What I'd like to know, though, is what *precisely* does this entail?'

'That you be ready when I come to collect you at six o'clock this evening.'

He shot to his feet. He needed to breathe in air that didn't smell of Caro. He needed to clear his head before he did something stupid.

She blinked. 'Where are we going?'

'You'll see.'

'What should I wear?'

He'd started to turn away. Gritting his teeth, he turned back and tried to give her a cursory once-over. But his hormones said *To hell with cursory* and he found himself taking his time. Her heightened colour told him she wasn't as averse to his gaze as she no doubt wished she were.

'What you're wearing now will do nicely.'

With a half-muttered expletive, he bent down and pressed his lips to hers, refusing to resist temptation a moment longer. The kiss lasted no longer than two beats of his heart—a brief press and a slight parting of his lips to shape his mouth to hers, a silent silky slide—and then he stepped away.

Stunned caramel eyes stared back at him.

'Please excuse me if I don't walk you home.'

Walking her home would be asking for trouble. He turned and left before he could say another word—before he did something dangerous like drag her to her feet and kiss her properly. One touch of his lips to hers hadn't eased the need inside him. It had turned it into a raging, roaring monster. Her scent and her softness had made him hungrier than he'd ever been in his life before. He needed to get himself back under control before their date tonight.

Caro changed from her earlier outfit of jeans and a peasant-style top into a pair of white linen trousers, and then flipped through her selection of blouses.

The blue silk, perhaps?

No, Jack had always loved her in blue. She didn't want him thinking she was dressing to please him.

The red?

Good Lord, no! She swished that along the rack. Red and sex were too closely aligned, and that wasn't the signal she wanted to send.

The black?

Low neckline—not a chance!

What about the grey?

She pulled it out, but shoved it back into the closet almost immediately. It showed too much midriff. She needed something asexual. She didn't want Jack kissing her again.

Liar.

Even if that lunchtime kiss had only been for show…in case anyone had been watching.

Don't be an idiot.

He'd kissed her because he'd wanted to. End of story.

A breath shuddered out of her, her fingers reaching up to trace her lips. Lips that remembered the touch and taste of him as if it had been only yesterday since she'd last kissed him. Lips that throbbed and burned with a violence she'd thought she'd managed to quell. That was bad news. *Very* bad news. She had to make sure he didn't kiss her again.

Or if he tried to she had to take evasive measures— not just sit there like a landed duck, waiting and hoping for it to happen.

Now choose a blouse!

In the end she decided on a soft pink button-down with a Peter Pan collar. As it wasn't fitted, no one could possibly accuse it of being sexy. With a sigh, she tugged it on. And not a moment too soon either, as Jack's knock sounded on the door while she was still buttoning it up.

How do you know it's Jack? It could be anyone.

She shook her head, slipping the strap of her purse over her shoulder. It would be Jack, all right. Nobody else knocked with quite the same authority. Besides, he was bang on time. He'd always had a thing for punctuality.

She took a deep breath and then opened the

door, immediately stepping outside and pulling the door closed behind her. She did *not* want Jack in her tiny flat again, with its temptation of a bedroom a mere door away. The less privacy Jack and she had, the better.

'Hello, Jack.' She prevented herself from adding a snippy *again* to her greeting.

'Caro.'

The heat from his body beat at her. He wore an unfamiliar aftershave, but it had the same invigorating effect as dark-roasted coffee beans. She breathed in deeply, her nose wrinkling in appreciation.

He gave her a flattering once-over. 'You changed.'

'Just freshened up.'

'You look nice.'

She went to say thank you, but he reached out to flick one of her buttons—the second button down...*the one right between her breasts*.

'These are kinda cute.'

She glanced down and then groaned. The buttons were bright red plastic cherries! 'If you knew the lengths I went to tonight to choose an appropriate shirt you'd laugh your head off.'

'Appropriate? You'd best share. I enjoy a good laugh.'

She moved them towards the elevator. 'I wanted to choose a shirt that was...demure.' She jabbed the elevator button and the door slid open.

'So I wouldn't kiss you again?' he said, ushering her inside and pushing the button for the ground floor.

She couldn't look at him. She moved her handbag from her right shoulder to her left. 'Something like that.'

'You hated it that much?'

'Can…can we continue this conversation once we're outside, please?'

They travelled the rest of the short distance in thin-lipped silence. At least, *his* lips were thin.

'You hated it that much?' he repeated, once they stood outside on the footpath.

She pulled in a breath of warm evening air. It didn't do much to clear her mind. 'No, Jack, the problem is that I liked it too much.'

He swung to stare at her, his lips going from thin-lipped sternness to erotic sensuality with a speed that had her tripping over her own feet. He reached out to steady her, but she held both hands up to ward him off. Although he didn't actually turn around and stare back the way they'd come, she could practically feel his mind moving back to her fifth-floor flat.

'Not going to happen,' she said, wishing her voice had emerged with a little more resolution.

'We still generate heat, kiddo.'

'What good did heat do us five years ago?'

A slow grin spread across his face, turning

him into a rakish pirate and her insides to molten honey. 'If I have to explain that to you then—'

'Hey, mister!' a taxicab driver shouted from the kerb. 'Do you want the cab or not?'

Caro gestured. 'Is that for us?'

Jack nodded.

She set off towards it at a half-trot. 'He wants it,' she called back to the driver, trying not to run. But she wanted to be away from her flat *now*.

Jack followed, a scowl darkening his features. He gave the driver directions, closed the dividing window and settled on the seat beside her.

'We're five years older and wiser, Caro.'

Older, maybe—but wiser? She wasn't so sure about that. 'What good do you think it would do us? We generate heat. So what? It's the kind that burns, and you know it.'

He stared down at his hands for a moment. 'Maybe this time we could make it work.'

Their marriage? She wanted to cover her ears. He *had* to be joking! She gave a hard shake of her head. 'No.'

His eyes flashed. 'You won't even think about it?'

She told herself that thin-lipped and forbidding was better than steamy sex-on-legs pirate. Not that she managed to convince herself about that.

She shook the thought away. 'Do you really believe I've been able to think of anything else since I saw you five days ago?'

She recognised the quickening in his eyes but she shook her head again, awash with a sorrow that had her wanting to curl up into a ball.

'Hell, Caro,' he ground out. 'Don't look at me like that.'

She dragged her gaze back to the front, not wanting to make him feel bad. She'd never wanted him to feel bad.

'Even though you told me you wanted a divorce, I haven't been able to stop wondering—what if we came to understand each other properly this time around? Could we make a go of it? Could this be the second chance I craved and fantasised about in those first few months after you left?'

Her throat closed over. Beside her, waves of tension rolled off Jack in a silent storm of turmoil. She passed a hand across her eyes and swallowed.

'The thing is, Jack, I keep circling back to the same conclusion. I don't believe I have what it takes to make you happy.'

'I—'

She held up a hand to cut him off. She met his gaze. 'And with you I would always be wondering… *Is he only with me because I agreed to have children?*'

He slumped back, pain tearing across his features, and she ached to hold him, to wipe that pain away and tell him that they could work it out—but if she did she feared she'd only hurt him worse later, and that would be unforgivable.

She forced herself to continue. 'I can't see things between us working out any better if *you* were the one to make the big sacrifice either. If we didn't have the children you want so much I'd be riddled with guilt.'

She clenched her purse in a death grip on her lap.

'I don't believe love and marriage should be all about self-sacrifice. It should be about two people making compromises, so they can both be happy.'

She didn't think that was possible in her and Jack's case.

'It's about both people being equally important.'

She tried, unsuccessfully, to unclench her hands from around her purse.

'I can't help feeling that in either scenario the things that drew you to me, the things you loved about me, would fade…and in the end you'd leave me anyway.' She stared at her hands. 'I'm not saying this to be mean. I'm saying it because this time I want to be completely honest with you.'

She finally turned to look at him. His eyes were alternately as soft as a kiss and as hard as adamantine.

His lips finally twisted with self-mockery. 'You really have thought about it, haven't you?'

She wanted to cry. When he'd come searching for closure had he pictured *this*?

He turned to gaze out of the window. 'No amount of mind-blowing sex can compete with that.'

A chasm opened up inside her. 'I wish I could have that great sex without paying the price.'

'But that wouldn't be the case. Not for either one of us.'

It helped a little to hear him admit it too. 'Some people subscribe to the view that the loving is worth the losing, but I don't believe that. It took me too long to get over you the last time, Jack. And I know now it was just as hard for you.'

'You don't want to risk it again?'

Did he? *He couldn't!* She shook her head. 'The odds are just too high.'

He took her hand, pressed it between both his own before lifting it to his lips and placing a kiss to her palm. Her blood danced and burned.

'I'm so sorry, Caro. For everything.'

The backs of her eyes stung. 'Me too.'

He laid her hand back in her lap with a gentleness that had her biting her lip. How could she still want to throw herself at him with such fierceness after the conversation they'd just had?

'I swear I won't kiss you again.'

She closed her eyes and concentrated on her breathing. 'Thank you.'

'I only want to make things easier for you. Better. It was all I ever wanted.'

She couldn't speak. She could only nod. She knew that too. It was why she'd fallen so hard for him in the first place.

The taxi stopped. Caro glanced at her watch. It felt as if a whole lifetime had passed, but in reality it had been only ten minutes. She slid out from the door Jack held open for her and waited as he paid the cab driver, pulling in deep breaths to try and calm the storm raging through her.

She'd hoped such a frank conversation would ease the storm. That wasn't going to be the case, evidently. She was at a loss as to what else to try.

She glanced around, searching for distraction. She'd paid next to no mind to where they'd been going, but their location looked vaguely familiar.

Jack moved up beside her. 'Do you know where we are?'

The taxi pulled away and drove off into the warm summer evening. She had no right to feel abandoned.

Huffing back a sigh, she pointed to a sign. 'That says this is Red Lion Square. So...we're in Holborn?'

He nodded. 'We're heading for a building on the other side of the park—and then my dastardly plan will be revealed.'

He smiled, but she saw the effort it cost him.

Reaching out, she pulled him to a halt. His warmth immediately flooded her, daring her to foolishness, and she reefed her hand back.

'Are…are you sure you still want to do this?' She wouldn't blame him if he wanted a time out. It wasn't his job to help her find happiness again, her relish for life.

'Of course I still want to do this.' He stared at her for a long moment before shoving his hands into his pockets. 'I have no desire, though, to force you into something *you* don't want to do. If you want to leave, Caro, just say the word.'

She didn't even know what *this* was yet, but that wasn't really what he was referring to anyway. He wanted to see her smile and have fun again. She wanted the same for him. And she sensed that by helping her he'd be helping himself.

From somewhere she dug out a smile. 'I'm game if you are.' The force of his smile was her reward. She turned away, blinking. 'Lead on, Macduff.'

He led her into the headquarters of one of London's premier Scrabble clubs. Her jaw dropped as she took in the sight of the boards and players set up around various tables.

A young man brimming over with energy came bustling up. 'You must be Caro Fielding. I'm Garry.' He turned to Jack. 'You're—?'

'A friend,' he supplied, with a wink at Caro. 'I rang yesterday.'

'I remember. You said Caro might be interested in joining our club.'

He had, had he? 'I—'

'She's a brilliant player,' Jack inserted.

Good grief! 'I haven't played in an age. And he exaggerates.' She elbowed Jack in the ribs but he just grinned down at her, utterly unrepentant.

'Well, why don't we set you up with Yvonne? She's pretty new to the club too.'

Before Caro knew it she found herself deep in a fierce game of Scrabble. She'd loved the game once. She and Jack used to play it—though he'd never really been a match for her. He'd only ever played to humour her. But when had *she* stopped playing?

When Jack had left.

Her heart thudded.

At the end of the game she sat back and stared at the neat rows of tiles. 'You just wiped the board with me.' A thread of competitiveness squirmed its way to the surface. 'Again?' She wanted a chance to redeem herself.

They started another game. Caro was vaguely aware of Jack strolling around the room, watching the other games, but she had to block him out to concentrate on the game in front of her.

'You might be rusty,' her opponent said, 'but you're picking it up again at a fast rate of knots.'

Caro lost the second game as well—but not by

a margin that made her wince. An old fire she'd forgotten kindled to life in her belly. 'Best of five?'

Yvonne simply grinned and started selecting a new set of tiles.

Caro was amazed to find that three hours had passed when a bell sounded and they were instructed to finish up their games. Where had the time gone?

She glanced about, searching for Jack. When she found him, leaning back in a chair at a neighbouring table, he grinned at her, making her heart pitter-patter.

'Ready?' he said, standing and ambling over to her.

'Just about. I have to hand in my registration form and pay my club dues.'

He started to laugh. 'You don't want to think about it for a bit, then?'

'Heavens, no.'

For some reason that only made his grin widen. 'Do you know they hold competitions—and there's a Scrabble league? Did you know there are world championships?'

'You have your eye on the main prize?'

'Not this year.' She tossed her head, a little fizz of excitement spiralling through her. 'But next year could be a possibility.'

'C'mon.' Throwing an arm across her shoulders, he led her outside. 'Let me buy you a burger.'

'Ooh, yes, please! I'm starved!'

'And I owe you a meal.' He grimaced down at her in apology. 'I didn't realise until much later that I'd left you holding the bill for lunch today.'

They both remembered the reason why Jack had left so abruptly.

He removed his arm from her shoulders and she edged away from him a fraction. She cleared her throat and tried to grab hold of the camaraderie that had wrapped itself around them so warmly just a few short moments ago.

'It's a small price to pay for this.' She gestured back behind her to indicate the Scrabble club. 'I had a great time tonight. I'd forgotten how much I enjoyed Scrabble. It was an inspired idea, Jack. Thank you.'

The burgers were delicious, but while they both did their best to make small talk the easy camaraderie had fled.

'Where are you staying?' she asked him afterwards.

He named a hotel in Covent Garden. 'Oh, Jack, you could walk there from here. Please—you don't need to see me home.'

'But—'

'Truly! I'd prefer it if you didn't.' She wanted to avoid any fraught goodnight moments on her doorstep. 'But I'd appreciate it if you'd flag me down a cab.'

'You insist?' he asked quietly.

She gave a quick nod. He looked far from happy, but he didn't argue. He hailed a cab and insisted on paying for it.

As he helped her inside he said, 'Tomorrow. Six p.m.'

A ripple of anticipation squirrelled through her. 'Again?'

'Wear a dress and heels. Small heels—not stilettos.'

She did everything she could to prevent her breath from hitching. 'Will we be cabbing it again?'

'Yes.'

'Then I'll wait downstairs for you. Goodnight, Jack.'

With that she sat back, before she did something daft…like kiss him.

CHAPTER SEVEN

'SALSA CLASSES?'

Caro's mouth dropped open, but Jack kept his concentration trained on the expressions flitting across her face rather than the temptation of her lips, shining with a rose-pink lipstick.

Lips he ached to kiss fully and very, *very* thoroughly. Lips he wanted to tease, tempt and taste. The longer he stared at those lips, the greater the need that built inside him.

Who was he trying to kid? What he wanted was Caro, warm and wild in his arms, wanting him just as much as he wanted her.

Except he wasn't supposed to be thinking about that!

He dragged his attention back to her expression, trying to decide whether she was excited or appalled. Maybe a bit of both.

'What do you think?' he found himself asking.

They'd attended dance classes once—back before they were married. At the time he hadn't been all that keen—except on the thought of holding Caro in his arms. He hadn't let on, though. He'd been too intent on wooing her. To his utter surprise, the dance classes had been a blast.

She frowned up at him. 'I'm really not sure this is such a good idea.'

She was afraid of the physicality of the dance, afraid of where it would lead…and maybe a little afraid of herself and her own body's yearnings. He needed to put her mind at rest and reassure her that they could survive one dance class together.

The results of the few enquiries he'd made into Caro's life since returning to London—showing the extent of her withdrawal into herself—had shocked him. That was the price she'd paid for the breakdown of their marriage. It was a price she should never have paid and it was time for it to stop.

He touched a finger to her temple—gently and very briefly. 'The Scrabble is for your mind and the dance classes are for your body. A healthy mind and a—'

She blew out a breath that made her fringe flutter. 'And a healthy body,' she finished for him. 'If you say one word about me eating too much cake…'

'Wouldn't dream of it. Cake is necessary too. I don't see why you should feel guilty about eating cake.'

She rolled her shoulders. 'I don't.'

'Then stop being so defensive.'

He moved them to one side as a couple bounded up the steps to push through the door.

The young woman turned just before entering. 'Are you thinking of joining the class? You should. It's great fun—and a really good workout.'

'My friend here is,' Jack said, before Caro could pooh-pooh the whole idea. 'The problem is that I can only attend tonight.'

'That's not a problem. There are two guys in the class who are currently looking for partners—Marcus and Timothy.' She leaned in closer. 'I'd go with Tim. He's a bit shy, but really lovely. See you inside.'

With a smile, she and her partner disappeared through the door.

Jack turned back to Caro and spread his hands, saying nothing, just letting the situation speak for itself. She bit her lip, glancing once again at the flyer on the door.

Her uncertainty pricked him. 'You loved dancing once.'

'Yes.'

He wanted to ask her what she was afraid of. He didn't. He decided to try and lighten the mood instead. 'It's either this or rock wall climbing.'

She spun back to him, her eyes widening. 'I beg your pardon?'

'There's a gym not too far from your flat that has a climbing wall. I bet it'd be great fun. A great workout for the arms too.'

A laugh shot out of her. 'You can't be serious?'

'Why not?' He grinned back at her. 'Except as we're here, and not there, I did come to the conclusion that you'd prefer this to that. If I'm wrong, just say the word.'

When had she become so risk-averse?

With another laugh, she took his arm and hauled him into the hall.

She wore an amber-coloured dress with a fitted bodice and a skirt that flared gently to mid-calf. It looked deceptively plain until she moved, and then the material—shot through with sparkling threads of gold and bronze—shimmered. Beneath the lights she sparkled, until he had to blink to clear his vision. He led her to a spot on the dance floor before moving away to speak to the dance instructor for a few moments.

He drew in a fortifying breath before returning to Caro and waiting for the class to begin.

He was insanely careful to keep a respectable distance between their bodies when the music started and the instructor began barking out instructions, but her warmth and her scent swirled up around him, playing sweet havoc with his senses. The touch of her hand in his, the feel of her through the thin material of her dress where his hand rested at her waist, sent a surge of hot possessiveness coursing through him.

He had no right to that possessiveness.

He gritted his teeth. He only had to get through one night of salsa. Just a single hour. He gritted his teeth harder. He could do it.

'I can't believe how quickly it's all coming back,' Caro murmured, swinging away and then swinging back.

Her throaty whisper told him that their proximity bothered her too. *That* didn't help. He pulled in a deep breath, but it only made him draw in more of her scent. That *really* didn't help. *Don't think about it.*

'I was worried your feet might be black and blue after an hour of dancing with me.'

'Liar! If you were worried about anybody's feet it was your own. You were always better at this than me.'

'Not true. I mastered the moves quicker, but once you had them down pat you were a hundred times better.'

Their gazes snagged and locked. They moved across the dance floor with an effortlessness that had Jack feeling as if they were flying. Staring into her dark caramel eyes, he could almost feel himself falling...

Stop! a voice screamed through his mind.

With a heart that beat too hard, he dragged his

gaze away. He had to swallow a couple of times before he trusted his voice to work. 'I checked with the teacher and found out that's Tim over there.' He nodded across the room to a slim, well-groomed man with light hair and a pleasant smile.

Caro mistimed her step and trod on Jack's foot. 'Oops.' She grimaced up at him in apology. 'It's a challenge to count steps, talk and look round all at the same time.'

Fibber. But he didn't call her on it.

'Why don't we introduce ourselves at the end of the lesson?'

One of her shoulders lifted. 'Seems to me he's found a partner.'

'She's an instructor here. She's filling in to make up the numbers.' He glanced across at the other man again. 'He seems pleasant enough. He's not tramping all over her feet either, so that's a plus.'

'For heaven's sake, Jack! Do you want to give him my phone number and set me up on a date with him too?'

He snapped back at her biting tone. 'Don't be ridiculous.' He glanced across at the other man again. This Tim wasn't her type…was he? 'Your private life is your own to do with as you will.'

It suddenly occurred to him that encouraging Caro to get out more would throw her into the company of men. Men who would ask her out. Men she might find attractive.

He had a sudden vision of Caro in the other man's arms and—

'Ouch!'

He pulled to an abrupt halt. 'Hell! Sorry!'

He bent down to rub her foot, but she pushed him away, glaring at him. 'What are you doing?'

'I was…um…going to rub it better.'

'Not necessary!'

Those amazing eyes of hers flashed cinnamon and gold fire and all he could think of was kissing her foot better, and then working his way up her leg and—'

'Come! Come!'

The dance instructor, who had a tendency to repeat everything twice, marched up to them now, clapping his hands, making Jack blink.

'You must concentrate! *Concentrate*, Jack. Take your partner in your arms.'

He adjusted their positions, moving them a fraction closer to each other, pressing a hand into the small of Caro's back to force her to straighten. The action thrust her chest towards Jack. Jack stared at those delectable curves, mere centimetres from his chest, and swallowed convulsively.

Good God! Torture. Utter torture.

'You must maintain eye contact,' the teacher barked at them.

With a superhuman effort Jack raised his eyes to Caro's.

'This is the salsa!' The man made an exaggerated gesture with his hands. 'This is the dance of flirtation!'

Caro's eyes widened. It was all Jack could do to swallow back a groan.

'So…you must flirt.' He performed another flourish. *'Flirt!'*

Caro's eyes started to dance, and Jack could feel answering laughter building inside him. The instructor moved away to harangue another couple.

'You *will* flirt,' Caro ordered in a mock authoritarian tone. 'We have ways of *making* you flirt!'

He gulped back a bark of laughter.

'It's quite a conundrum,' Caro continued, this time in her own voice. 'How exactly *does* one flirt while dancing?'

She made her eyes innocent and wide. Too innocent. He felt suddenly alive.

He grinned and nodded towards their teacher. 'According to him, lots of eye contact.'

She eyeballed Jack, making him laugh. 'Tick,' she said. 'We have that down pat. But we can't accidentally brush fingers when we're already holding hands.'

'And with your hands already engaged you can't do that cute twirling of your hair around one finger thing, while giving me a come-hither look.'

She snorted back a laugh. 'Ah, but I *can* lasciviously lick my lips in a suggestive fashion.'

She proceeded to do so—but she did it in such an over the top fashion he found himself hard pressed not to dissolve into laughter.

'Your turn,' she instructed. 'You *will* flirt!'

He copied her move in an even more exaggerated way, until they were laughing so hard they had to hold onto each other to remain upright.

'Excellent! Excellent!' The instructor beamed at them. 'Now, *dance.*'

The rest of the hour flew by.

'That was fun,' Caro said a little breathlessly when they stood on the footpath outside afterwards.

Jack put her breathlessness down to the unaccustomed exercise.

'Night, Tim,' she called out when the other man bounded down the steps.

'See you next week, Caro,' the other man called back, with a smile that set Jack's teeth on edge.

He refused to put Caro's breathlessness down to the fact she'd made a *new friend.*

'Stop glaring like that,' Caro chided. 'It was your idea.'

Not one of his better ones, though. It felt as if he was handing her over to another man. Without a fight.

He scowled up at the sky. 'Just remember I don't want an invitation to your wedding.'

'I'm not even going to dignify that with an answer.'

He shook himself. He wouldn't blame her for simply walking away. 'Sorry. Uh...hungry?'

She eyed him for a moment before finally nodding. 'Yes.'

Excellent! He refused to dwell on why he wasn't ready for the night to end. 'There's a great little restaurant around the corner that has—'

'No.'

He frowned at her. 'No?'

'A restaurant meal is too much like a date, Jack, and we aren't dating. C'mon—I know a better place.'

The dance school was in Bermondsey, just a couple of stops on the tube from Caro's nearest station. He'd chosen it for the convenience of its location. He'd wanted to make attending classes there as easy and trouble-free for her as possible. He scowled down at his feet. He hadn't meant for it to be that easy for her to hook up with another man, though.

He tried to shrug the thought off. It shouldn't matter to him. He wanted a divorce, remember?

Ten minutes later he found himself in a large park, with people dotting the green space, making the most of the summer evening.

She pointed. 'There.'

He grimaced. 'A fish and chip van?'

'You can get a burger if you prefer.'

Without further ado she marched up to the van and ordered a single portion of fish and chips. She shook her head when he reached for his wallet. She paid for it herself. She didn't offer to pay for his meal.

He received the message loud and clear.

He ordered the same, and then found them a vacant park bench. He figured her dress wasn't made for sitting on the grass.

'So, if this isn't a date,' he said, unwrapping his fish and chips, 'what is it?'

'The kind of meal friends would share.'

Was this how she and Tim would start out— sharing a friendly meal in the park? Maybe they'd eventually progress to dinner in a pub, and then romantic candlelit dinners for two in posh restaurants?

Stop it! Caro deserves to be happy.

He closed his eyes. She *did* deserve to be happy.

'Are you okay?' she asked quietly.

It was one of the things he'd always appreciated about her—she never made a fuss, never drew attention unnecessarily.

He shook his head, and then nodded, and finally shrugged, feeling oddly at sea. 'I wanted to say that I've thought about what you said the other day.'

'Hmm...?' She popped a chip into her mouth. 'You might need to be a bit more specific than that.'

'About my reasons for wanting children.'

She paused with a chip halfway to her mouth. 'You don't have to explain anything to me, Jack.'

'If not to you, then who?'

She lowered the chip back to the packet. 'To yourself.'

He stared around the park, at the family groups dotted here and there, and his soul yearned towards them. To belong like that, to be loved like that...to *create* that—it was all he'd ever really wanted.

He turned back to Caro. 'It's occurred to me that I'm better prepared for fatherhood now than I was five years ago. You were right. I wanted children too much back then.'

'I'm not sure it's possible to want something like that *too* much,' she said carefully.

'You were spot-on. I wanted them for *me*—to make me feel better and...and whole.'

She stilled, staring down at the food in her lap. 'Even if that was the case, I don't doubt that you'd have been a fabulous father.'

'Maybe—but I'd have had a few rude awakenings along the way.'

She went back to eating. 'That's just life.'

'I wanted you to know that, after looking back, I don't blame you for the misgivings you had.'

She slumped, as if her spine no longer had the strength to support her. She stared at him, her eyes sparking copper and gold. 'That…' She swallowed. 'Thank you. That… It means a lot.'

She deserved to be happy.

He forced himself to continue. 'You've also made me confront my own selfishness.'

Her head rocked back.

'When I said I wanted to have a family, what I really wanted was for you to *give* me a family. I expected you to give up work and be a full-time mother.' He stared down at his hands. 'But if someone had asked *me* to give up everything I was asking you to give up when I was twenty-five, I wouldn't have given it up without a fight either. I'm…I'm sorry I asked that of you.'

She reached out to grip his hand. She didn't speak until he turned to look at her. 'What you wanted wasn't a bad thing, Jack. Stop beating yourself up about it. Apology accepted, okay?'

Her words and her smile made him feel lighter. She released his hand and it took all his strength not to reach for her again.

'Wow…' She shook her head. 'When you say you want closure you really mean it, huh?'

He didn't want closure. He wanted her back.

The knowledge he'd been trying to ignore for two days pounded through him now.

'For my part...' She pushed her shoulders back. 'I'm sorry I withdrew into myself the way I did. I should've tried to talk to you more, explained how I was feeling. You're not a mind reader. It was unfair of me.'

But she'd been scared—scared that he'd reject her. Just as she was too scared to take a chance on them again now.

'I am truly sorry for that, Jack.'

'Likewise—apology accepted.'

Could he change her mind? His heart beat hard. Could he find a way to make her fall in love with him again? What about the issue of children? Could he give that dream up for Caro?

Caro tried to ignore how hard her heart burned at the careworn, almost defeated expression on Jack's face.

She tried to dredge up a smile. 'We're a classic example of marry in haste, repent at leisure.'

They should have made more time to get to know each other on an intellectual level, discussed what they wanted out of life. Instead they'd trusted their instincts—had believed so strongly that they were fated for each other. Because that was what it had felt like—and they'd ignored everything else.

Being with Jack had felt so *right*. The world had

made sense in a way it never had before. The fact of the matter, though, was that their instincts had led them astray. They'd wanted to believe so badly in the rightness and the *uniqueness* of their love that they'd left logic, clear thinking and reality behind. Arrogant—that was what they'd been… too arrogant.

'You don't believe what's been broken can be fixed, do you?'

He was talking about *them*. Her stomach churned. He wasn't thinking clearly—muddled by a combination of hormones, nostalgia and an aching sentimentality that she could—unfortunately—relate to. The fact that he found himself liking her again had rocked him—shocked him to his marrow. It was no surprise to her that she still liked *him*.

She glanced across and a chasm of yearning opened up inside her. Not liking each other would make things so much easier. If only…

She bit back a sigh. No, she couldn't think like that. One of them had to keep a clear head.

'No.' She made herself speak clearly and confidently. 'I don't believe we can be fixed.'

His shoulders slumped and it took all of Caro's strength not to lean across and hug him, unsay her words. Jack hated failure. He always had. But in a day or two he'd see that she was right—that she was saving both of them from more heartbreak.

'Eat your chips,' she ordered. 'They'll make you feel better.'

He cocked a disbelieving eyebrow. 'Chips will make me *feel better*?'

'Deep-fried carbohydrate cannot help but boost the soul.'

Five years ago Jack had left angry—in a white-hot fury. And he'd stayed angry for all this time. It was what had fuelled him. Now that the anger was dissipating it was only natural that he should find himself grieving for their lost love. She'd already done her grieving. He was just catching up.

It was odd, then, how she found herself wanting to be there for him as he went through it.

Dangerous.

The word whispered through her and she acknowledged its innate truth. She had to be careful not to get sucked back into the disaster their marriage had become. She couldn't go through that a second time.

She went back to diligently eating her chips. Wallowing wouldn't do either one of them any good. What they needed was a sharp reminder of their differences.

'You know,' she started, with a sidelong glance in his direction, 'I always envied your confidence that you could make a family work.'

His gaze grew keener. 'What do you mean?'

She munched a chip, desperately searching for a

carbohydrate high. 'My own experience of family wasn't exactly positive. It didn't provide me with role models of any note.' She gave a short laugh. 'Let's be frank, it was totally dysfunctional. You met my father. For as long as I can remember he was remote and controlling. Paul tells me he was different when my mother was alive, but…'

'You don't believe that?'

She shrugged. 'I don't have any strong memories of my mother before she died.'

'You were only five.'

'In the same vein, I don't have any memories of my father being different before she died.' She couldn't recall *ever* connecting emotionally with him. 'Although I don't doubt her death affected him.'

Her mother had died of breast cancer, and she knew, because Paul had told her, that her mother had been seriously ill for the eight months prior to her death. It must have been hell to witness.

She shook herself and glanced at Jack. The look in his eyes made her mouth suddenly dry and she didn't know why.

'You think he loved her?' he asked.

She tried to get her pulse back under control. 'I guess the fact it took him fourteen years to re-marry is probably testament to that.'

He frowned. 'You're saying you think you'd

take some of that dysfunction into your relationship with any children you might have?'

'Well…yes. It seems plausible doesn't it? I mean, in my kinder moments I tell myself my father was simply a product of his own upbringing…'

'But doesn't the fact that you're aware of that mean you'll take extra steps to make sure you're *not* like him?'

She shoved a chip into her mouth and chewed doggedly. 'I don't know. It all seems such a… *gamble*.'

What if she couldn't help it? What if she made those hypothetical children's lives a misery? The thought made her sick to the stomach.

She turned to face him more fully. 'Jack, your childhood was far worse than mine.'

He shook his head. 'I'm not so sure about that.'

'I grew up with wealth. Money makes a big difference. It couldn't buy me a family, granted,' she added, when he went to break in. 'But it was a hundred times better than being in the same situation and struggling financially. A *thousand* times better. I've been lucky in a lot of ways.'

Lucky in ways Jack had never been. She'd done nothing to earn those advantages. He'd deserved so much better from life.

He'd deserved so much better from her.

'You think my confidence is misplaced?'

'No!' She reached out to grip his arm, horrified that he'd interpreted her words in such a way. 'I *always* believed you'd be a wonderful father. I just wished I could believe in my own abilities so wholeheartedly. That's what I meant when I said I envied you. I…I didn't understand where that confidence came from. I still don't.'

He glanced down at her hand. She reefed it back into her lap, heat flushing through her. 'I…uh… sorry.'

'You don't need to apologise for touching me, Caro. I like you touching me.'

His words slid over her like warm silk, and for a moment all she could do was stare at him. Her breathing became shallow and laboured. Had he gone mad? She eyed him uncertainly before shuffling away a few centimetres. He couldn't be suggesting that they…?

Don't be daft. He'd promised to not kiss her again. *You didn't promise not to kiss him, though.*

She waved a hand in front of her face.

Jack scrunched up what was left of his dinner and tossed it into a nearby bin. His every movement reminded her of his latent athleticism. He'd always been fit and physical, and he'd been very athletic in bed.

Don't think about that now.

He settled back, stretching his legs out in front of him and his arms along the back of the bench.

His fingers toyed with her hair. He tugged on it gently and she tried not to jump.

'There was one particular foster family that I stayed with when I was twelve...'

She stilled. Jack had rarely spoken about his childhood, or about growing up in foster homes. All that she knew was that his mother had been a drug addict who'd died from an overdose when Jack was four. But whenever she'd asked him questions or pressed him for more information, he'd become testy. The most she'd ever extracted from him was that he hadn't suffered any particular cruelties, but he hadn't been able to wait until he was an adult, when he could take charge of his own life.

As for the rest of it... She'd automatically understood his loneliness in the same way he'd understood hers.

'What was this family like?' She held her breath and waited to see if he would answer.

'They were everything I ever dreamed a family could be.' He smiled, his gaze warm, and it made something inside her stir to life. 'Through them I glimpsed what family could be. Living with them gave me hope.'

Hope?

He told her how Darrel and Christine Jameson hadn't been able to have children of their own, so they'd fostered children in need instead. He described picnics and outings and dinner times around the kitchen table when the television would be turned off and they'd talk—telling each other about their day. He laughed as he told her about being grounded when he'd played hooky from school once, and being nagged to clean his room. He sketched portraits of the two foster brothers he'd had there, and how for twelve short months he'd felt part of something bigger than himself—something good and worthwhile.

Something he'd spent the rest of his life trying to recapture, she realised now.

Envy swirled up through her. Envy and longing. 'They sound wonderful. Perfect.'

'They were going to adopt me.'

Her heart dipped and started to throb. This story didn't have a happy ending.

'What…what happened?' She had to force the words out. Jack had deserved to spend the rest of his life enfolded within this family's embrace. Why hadn't that happened?

'Darrel and Christine were tight with a core group of other foster carers.'

That sounded like a *good* thing. They'd have provided each other with support and advice.

'One of their friends' foster sons got into some serious trouble—taking drugs, stealing cars.'

Her heart thumped.

'It was a mess. He became violent with his foster mother.'

She pulled in a jagged breath. 'That's awful.'

'Nobody pretends that taking on a troubled child is going to be easy, but common wisdom has it that the good gained is worth the trouble and the heartache.'

'You don't believe that?'

He pulled in a breath. 'Seems to me that all too often "well-intentioned" and "idealistic" are merely synonyms for "naive" and "unprepared".'

She swallowed, wanting to argue with him but sensing the innate truth of his words.

'The incident really spooked them—especially Christine. And when my older foster brother was caught drinking alcohol, we were all farmed back to Social Services.'

Although he didn't move, the bleakness in his eyes told her how that had devastated him.

She pressed a hand to her mouth for a moment. 'I'm so sorry.'

He shrugged, and she didn't know how he managed to maintain such an easy, open posture. All she wanted to do was fling herself against his chest and sob for the thirteen-year-old boy who'd lost the family of his dreams. She could feel his fingers in her hair, as if touching it brought him some measure of comfort. She held still, willing him to take whatever comfort he could.

'You never found another family like that one?'

He cocked an eyebrow. 'How do I grieve, Caro?'

She stared at him and then nodded. 'You get angry.'

'I stayed angry for the next five years. I acted out. Got a name for myself within the system. I spent my last two years in a group home.'

She swallowed. 'A detention centre?'

'No, it wasn't that bad, but it wasn't really a…a *home*, if you catch my drift.'

She did. And everything inside her ached for him.

'It was a place to mark time until I became an adult and the state could wash its hands of me.'

She tried to control the rush of anger that shook through her. 'Boarding school was a hundred times better than that!'

He twisted a strand of her hair around his fingers. 'I'm glad.'

She bit her lip, the touch of his hand in her hair sending spirals of pleasure gyrating deep in her belly. She shifted in an attempt to relieve the ache. 'Why aren't you bitter about losing that family?'

'I was for a long time, but they taught me that my dream could come true. I'll always be grateful to them for that—for providing me with a yardstick I could cling to.'

She moistened her lips. He zeroed in on the action, his eyes darkening, and a groan rose up through her. The pulse at the base of his jaw started to pound and her heart surged up into her throat to hammer in time with it. She tried to draw a steadying breath into her lungs, but all she drew in was the scent of him.

'Have you...have you ever considered becoming a foster carer yourself?'

His fingers in her hair stilled. 'No.'

'Maybe you should. You'd know the pitfalls and understand the stumbling blocks. You'd be brilliant.'

He'd be a wonderful father.

'I...'

He faltered and she shrugged. 'It's just something to think about. Obviously not the kind of decision you'd make on the spur of the moment.'

'But worth considering,' he agreed slowly.

She had no intention of wasting such a rare opportunity when he was in such an amenable mood. 'So you didn't feel you belonged anywhere again until you joined the police force?'

When she'd first met Jack he'd been working for the Australian Federal Police. He'd been stationed in London, on secondment to the British Intelligence Service as a surveillance instructor.

Those blue eyes of his sparked and grew even keener if that were at all possible. 'The police force gave me a direction in life. But, Caro, I didn't feel I belonged anywhere again until I met *you*.'

CHAPTER EIGHT

CARO'S MOBILE PHONE RANG, making her jump. Her fountain pen corkscrewed across the page in an example of less than elegant penmanship. She glared at the blot of ink she'd left behind. *Botheration!*

The phone rang again. She pressed it to her ear. 'Hello?'

'Are you home?'

Her hand about the phone tightened. 'Good morning, Jack. How are you? I'm well. Thank you for asking.'

His chuckle curled her toes. 'Caro, as ever, it's a delight.'

She wanted to stretch and purr at the warm amusement in his voice. *So* not good.

'I'm running up your stairs as we speak.'

He didn't sound the slightest bit breathless. If she walked, let alone jogged up the stairs, she'd huff and puff for a good five minutes.

'Really, Jack, is running necessary?'

This time he laughed outright.

Don't bask. Stop basking!

'Your door has just come into view.'

She snapped her phone off and turned to stare at her door. What was he doing here? If they had to meet, why couldn't they have done it somewhere public?

The snuffbox!

Her stomach tightened. With reluctant legs, but a madly beating heart, she moved across to the door and opened it. She tried not to look at him too squarely as she ushered him in. 'To what do I owe the pleasure?'

'Your manners are one of the things I've always admired about you, Caro.'

Was he laughing at her? Or did he sense her resentment at his intrusion? 'Do you have news about the snuffbox? Have there been any developments?'

He glanced down at the table and frowned. 'What are you doing?'

A scowl she didn't understand started to build inside her. She swallowed and sat. 'You're the detective. What do you *think* I'm doing?'

He lifted the sheet of paper she'd been practising on. '"*My darling Barbara. Wishing you many happy returns for the day. May you always be happy. To my darling wife. Love. Much love. All my love. Roland.*"' He turned the paper sideways to follow her scrawls. *"'Your Roland. Roland. Your loving husband, Roland.'"*

She grimaced. Would her father ever have signed himself as Barbara's loving husband? How on earth could she gush it up a little and still sound sincere?

Jack set the sheet of paper down and lifted one of the letters her father had sent to her while she'd been away at university. She'd received one or two missives from him every semester. Cursory things that never actually said much. She didn't even know why she'd kept them.

Dropping the letters back to the table, he reached for the jewellery catalogue and sales receipt sitting nearby. His nostrils flared, but whether at the picture of the diamond necklace or at the amount on the receipt, she wasn't sure.

'That is worth…'

'A significant amount of money,' she agreed.

'It's hideous.'

'Very true. However, it's not its beauty that matters, but its value.' Besides, it was the kind of piece her father would have admired. If he'd still been alive to admire it, that was.

Jack tossed the catalogue and the receipt back to the table. 'My detective brain informs me that it's Barbara's birthday soon.'

'Today.'

'And that you're faking a gift to her from your father…from beyond the grave.'

She summoned up her brightest smile. 'I *knew* you were more than just a pretty face.'

He didn't smile back. 'When were you going to tell me about this?'

His lips thinned when she blinked. She pushed her bangle up her arm. 'I wasn't. I don't see how it has any bearing on...on other things.'

'You try and guilt Barbara into giving the snuff-box back and you don't think that's relevant?'

No, she wasn't! This—

'How much more is this worth than the snuff-box?'

She could tell from the way he'd started to shake that he was getting a little...um...worked up. 'It's...' She moistened her lips. 'It's probably worth about three times as much, but that's beside the point. I—'

'You really think Barbara is the kind of woman who can be worked on like this? Have you lost your mind completely? She'll take the necklace *and* the snuffbox and run!'

Caro shot to her feet. 'Stop talking about her like that!' She strode around the table and stabbed a finger at his chest. 'You're wrong! I know her far better than you do, and yet you automatically assume your assessment of her is the right one and that mine is wrong!'

'You're too close.' The pulse at the base of his

jaw ticked. 'Your emotions are clouding your judgment.'

'No!' she shot back. 'It's your prejudices that are colouring your judgment. You're just like my father.' She whirled away. 'You think because Barbara is young and beautiful she must've married my father for his money.'

'If your father thought that, then why the hell did he marry her?'

She swung back. 'He didn't think that about her. He thought it about *you*!'

A silence suddenly descended around them. All that could be heard was the harsh intake of their breath.

Caro forced herself to continue. 'When you married me, you married a potential heiress. There are some people who would insinuate that your showing up now, like you have, is so you can collect your cut of the spoils. That's how people like my father and his lawyers think.'

His eyes grew so glacial the very air grew chill. 'I thought we'd already covered this.'

'I *don't* think like that. I *don't* believe you ever married me for my money and I *don't* believe money is the reason you're back in London. Why do I think that? Ooh, let's see…' She cocked her head to one side and lifted a finger to her chin. 'Could it be because I'm a good judge of character?'

Jack closed his eyes and dragged a hand down his face.

'Believe me, Jack. If there's one person who clouds my judgment, it's you. Not Barbara. I *know* she didn't marry my father for his money.'

He slammed his hands to his hips. 'But you believe she stole the snuffbox?'

'Not out of malice or for vengeance! It was a stupid spur-of-the-moment thing, done in a fit of pique and hurt, and now... Well, I expect she's bitterly regretting it and trying to find a way to get it back to me.'

He blew out a breath. 'May I sit?'

Good Lord, where were her manners? 'Please.' She gestured to a chair.

He fell into it and then motioned to the paraphernalia on the table. 'And this?'

She lowered herself back to her own chair. 'This has nothing to do with the rest of it.'

'I don't understand.'

She could tell from the low timbre of his voice that he wanted to. She moistened her lips. It meant talking about love. And talking about love to Jack...

She pushed her shoulders back. 'Believe me when I tell you that Barbara loved my father. She believed that he loved her too.'

It took a moment or two, but comprehension

eventually dawned across his face. 'And when he cut her out of his will…?'

She nodded. 'I mean, *we* know the reason for his sudden coldness.'

'But she has no idea he thought she was stealing from him?'

'I can't tell her the truth. She and Paul have no warmth for each other. With him, I fear she would retaliate. To be honest, a part of me wouldn't blame her.'

'Damn it, Caro. Part of me wants to say not your monkeys. Not your circus.'

'But it's not true, is it? I know they're not the kind of family you've always dreamed about, but they're all I have.'

Jack lifted the sheet of paper she'd been working on, stared at it with pursed lips. 'You're pretty good, you know.'

'Yes, I developed quite the reputation among my school friends.'

He glanced up, his eyes alive with curiosity. 'You'll have to tell me about it one day.'

When? At the end of the week he'd be gone and she'd never see him again. There wouldn't be any cosy nights in, laughing over reminiscences. Not for them.

'You're hoping this necklace will reinforce the fact that your father did love her?'

'Yes.'

He stared at the sundry messages she'd written when copying her father's handwriting. 'Men are less verbose than women.'

She leaned towards him. 'What are you trying to say?'

'I think you should just sign the card *Love, Roland* and leave it at that—leave all of this other stuff out.'

'Are you sure?'

'Positive.'

She glanced through the letters her father had sent her and realised Jack was right. Her father had never been demonstrative. At least not in his letters. Pulling the card towards her, she carefully wrote *Love, Roland.*

'Utterly authentic,' Jack said.

'It seems I've developed an unfortunate taste for deception. I've made the jeweller swear on all he holds dear that should Barbara contact him he'll say he was acting on my father's wishes—that all this was organised months before he died.'

'You've covered all bases?'

She hoped so. 'All I have to do now is drop this card in at the jeweller's and the package will be ready for delivery this afternoon.'

He stared at her for a long moment, making the blood pump faster around her body. It took a concerted effort not to fidget.

'What?'

'You're a woman of hidden talents, and at the moment that's to our advantage.'

'What are you talking about?'

'Can you forge Barbara's signature as well as you do your father's?'

'I don't know. I've never tried.' She'd never had to forge her stepmother's signature on a permission slip. Not that it had ever really been necessary to forge her father's either. It had just been easier than asking him—quicker and cleaner. It had saved her from having to look into his face and be confronted anew with his disappointment.

She pushed the thought away and pursed her lips. 'From memory, though, Barbara's isn't a difficult signature.' Unlike her father's, which was all bold strokes and angry slashes. 'I'd have to see it again before...'

She trailed off when he whipped out a form. Barbara's signature appeared at the bottom.

'Right...' She stared at it. After five attempts she had it down pat. 'How is this going to help us?'

He pulled a key from his pocket and set it on the table. 'Do you know what this is?'

'A key, obviously, but I have no idea what it's supposed to unlock.'

'A safety deposit box.'

She pulled in a quick breath. 'Barbara's?'

He nodded and handed her the appropriate paperwork.

'Good Lord, Jack! Where on earth did you get this?'

He raised an eyebrow and she held both hands up, palm outwards.

'You're right. I don't want to know.' She studied the paperwork. 'This isn't held at the bank my father did business with.' Her father had dealt with a bank in the city. This branch was in Chelsea.

'Do you know anyone who works there?'

She stared at the name of the bank and nodded. 'Lawrence Gardner—in another branch of the same bank. He's the father of an old school friend.' She shook her head. 'I'm sorry, Jack, but I can't ask him to check this safety deposit box. I—'

'What I'm trying to assess is the likelihood of us running into anyone you know if we were to go to that branch with you posing as Barbara.'

'I… What? Oh, God! I think I'm going to hyperventilate.'

He didn't turn a hair. 'We have two days to reclaim the snuffbox.'

Two days before a police inquiry descended on her head.

Caro swallowed. Barbara might have made a mistake, but she didn't deserve a police record and jail. 'You think the snuffbox is in that safety deposit box?'

'I can't think where else it'd be.'

'But…but I don't even *look* like Barbara,' she croaked. Barbara was tall, thin…gorgeous.

'You're both blonde.'

'She's ash-blonde.' Caro was a honey-blonde. 'And her hair is long.' So were her legs…

'I can get you a wig. And if you wore one of those sharp little power skirts she fancies, with a twinset and dark glasses…'

'Those things won't make me tall and thin.'

'No, the disguise won't hold up to close scrutiny,' he agreed. 'Not for someone who knows you or her…like this Lawrence Gardner. Would he recognise you?'

'Oh, that won't be a problem. He works from the bank's main office, which is in Knightsbridge.'

Her heart pounded hard.

She stared at him. 'You believe that if I go in there with this key, the ability to forge Barbara's signature and a blonde wig that I could pass for her?'

'Especially if you have some additional ID.' He handed her a credit card and an ATM card.

She squished her eyes shut. 'I'm not going to ask…'

'I'll have them back to her before she even knows they're missing.'

She hoped he was right.

'But, yes, I believe all of those things combined will gain us access to the box…if you dare.'

The way he said it reminded her of the way he'd challenged her on not having fun any more, on being *risk averse*. She pushed up her chin. She wanted that snuffbox back. She wanted Barbara in the clear. She dragged in a breath. *And* she wanted to keep her job and her professional reputation.

She folded her arms. Mostly to hide how badly her hands were shaking. 'When do we do it?'

'Today.'

Dear Lord!

Nerves jangled in Caro's stomach when Jack switched off the car's engine. She pulled down the sun visor to scrutinise her reflection in the mirror again.

'You look perfect,' he assured her.

He'd parked in an underground car park not too far from the bank. He didn't want to rely on taxis or public transport. He didn't want them to be seen. Which made her nerves jangle harder.

She pushed the visor back into place. 'I've been thinking. I should go in on my own.'

If she didn't pull this off then at least Jack wouldn't get into trouble too. She refused to dwell too deeply on the kind of trouble *she* could get into if this didn't go to plan. If she did that she'd freeze.

'Not a chance, kiddo. I'm in charge of this operation. I'm not sending you in there alone.'

She wanted to weep in relief. *Coward.*

'I'm not letting you have all the fun.'

She turned to gape at him. *'Fun?'*

'You and me—we're partners in crime.'

'Fun?' she repeated. *'Crime?'*

He grinned, exhilaration rippling in the depths of his eyes. 'Besides, we're not doing anything wrong. Not really.'

'Tell that to the judge.'

His grin widened. 'We don't want to steal anything. We don't want to hurt anyone. We just want to right a wrong.'

His words made her feel like a cross between Robin Hood and the Scarlet Pimpernel.

'To achieve that end we have to pit ourselves against the system—a worthy adversary. Are you going to tell me you're not experiencing even the tiniest flicker of anticipation?'

'Adrenaline junkie,' she accused, but there was no denying the fever that seemed to be working its way through her blood. *Keep breathing.* 'Any last instructions?'

'Do your best to channel Barbara.'

'That won't be difficult, darling.'

'Perfect.' He rubbed his hands together. 'Once inside, try and keep your head down. Stare at your hands or feign preoccupation with the contents of your purse. I don't want the CCTV cameras getting a good shot of you.'

Dear Lord!

* * *

There were two people ahead of her in the queue, and Caro's nerves steadied as they waited their turn. The fact that no alarms or sirens had sounded when they'd entered through the bank's sliding glass doors helped.

She twirled the wedding band Jack had suggested she wear round and round her finger. *Her* wedding band. She'd taken it off two years after Jack had left. Wearing it again now, she felt as if a missing part of her had been reclaimed. Which was an utterly crazy notion, because the thin circle of gold was nothing more than an empty symbol.

Don't think about it. Stay in character.

She pursed her lips and tapped her foot. She didn't watch a lot of thrillers, preferring dramas and comedies, but she did her best to summon a list of kick-ass heroines to mind. There was that Lara Croft *Tomb Raider* character—she was pretty handy in a tight situation. Oh, and Julia Roberts's character in *Ocean's Eleven*—very suave. They were women who strode out confidently and held their heads high.

She was about to toss her hair and lift her head when she recalled Jack's strictures to keep her head down. Hmm, on second thoughts they might not be the best archetypes to use as models in this particular situation. Still, she made a resolution to watch more movies with capable, efficient, devil-may-care, thrill-seeking female protagonists. And now that she thought about it, amateur dramatics might be a spot of fun. Maybe she should look into—

'We're up.'

She started at Jack's words, but her preoccupation helped her not only to keep her legs steady, but her voice steady too. 'Good afternoon,' she greeted the teller. 'I'd like to access my security deposit box, please.'

She handed over the paperwork Jack had procured. Heaven only knew when or how he'd done it, but she had visions of him dressed in black, prowling silently through the house in Mayfair.

Mind you, the vision wasn't without merit...

'If you'd like to follow me, Mrs Fielding?'

A thrill shot through her. This was working! They were going to get away with it.

'Certainly,' she said, following the teller along the length of the counter to a door. This was almost too easy. It occurred to her then that she could become a bit of an adrenaline junkie too.

The teller had started to punch in the door's code when it opened from the other side and a man strode out. Caro's heart leapt into her throat. She ducked her head, using Jack's body as a shield.

Please, please, please...

'Caro!'

Her heart thundered so hard she thought her

whole body must pulse with the force. What on earth was Lawrence doing *here*?

The teller frowned and glanced down at the paperwork. 'Caro...?'

Think fast!

'Lawrence, darling, it's *Barbara*.' She made herself beam. 'You do that every single time— mix me up with Caro. We're not even related. It must be the blonde hair.' She reached up to kiss his cheek. 'Please don't give me away...' she whispered. Throwing herself on her sword was the only option.

He stared at her for a long moment, before taking her hand and bringing it to his lips. 'That was clumsy of me. How have you been coping since the funeral?'

To Caro's utter horror she could feel tears start to prick the backs of her eyes. She gave an awkward shrug. 'Oh...you know.'

'What are you here for?'

Caro let the teller explain, while she tried to gain control over the pounding of her heart. What on earth was Lawrence doing in Chelsea rather than Knightsbridge?

'I'll take care of Ms Fielding,' Lawrence told his underling.

Caro swallowed a wince at Lawrence's use of Ms rather than Mrs.

Taking Caro's arm, he led her and Jack back

the way he'd come, not releasing her until they reached an office. He closed the door before swinging back. 'Caroline Elizabeth Fielding, what on *earth* do you think you're playing at?'

She swallowed. 'Hello, Uncle Lawrence.'

Uncle Lawrence! Jack closed his eyes. What on earth had he got Caro into?

He cleared his throat and stepped forward. 'Sir—'

'Uncle Lawrence, this is my husband, Jack. I don't believe the two of you ever met.'

As she spoke she led Jack to a chair and pressed him down into it. She squeezed his shoulder briefly—a not so-subtle signal to keep his mouth shut. Jack fully intended on taking the complete blame for whatever trouble was about to rain down on their heads, but he'd let her have her way for the moment. He was curious to see what she'd do.

'Jack, this is my Uncle Lawrence. It's an honorary title, of course.' In the same fashion as she'd led Jack to a chair she now led her 'honorary uncle' to the chair on the other side of the desk. 'He's my best friend's father. I spent most of my summers at their house in the Lake District.'

Her best friend? He thought for a moment. 'Suzie?'

Her eyebrows shot up as she took the seat beside him. 'You remember her?'

'Sure I do—the super-smart brunette addicted to *Twilight* movies and Hobnob biscuits.'

She'd been at their wedding. He frowned, trying hard to remember something else—anything else. If they could soften the father through the daughter...

'Wasn't she relocating to Switzerland, to run a department of some trading bank?'

Both Caro and Lawrence laughed. 'She's practically running the entire operation now,' her father said with pride, and Jack gave thanks for the tack Caro had taken.

'Good for her. I'm glad she's doing so well.'

'Well, she is now,' Caro said. 'Things were a bit bumpy there for a while, after her second little girl was born. Suzie had postnatal depression, but she's doing great again now.' She shot Lawrence a smile. 'We had a long, slightly wine-fuelled chat the week before last. She's doing wonderfully. You must be so proud of her.'

'I am.' He paused, his eyes keen. 'You know I'll always be grateful to you, Caro, for taking leave like you did, to be with her for those first few weeks after she was released from hospital. It made all the difference.'

It struck Jack how much pressure career-minded women who wanted children were put under. Men rarely suffered the same pressures. He eyed Caro now, his lips pursed.

'It's what friends do…and godmothers.'

Caro was a *godmother*?

'I'd do anything for Suzie and her family. Just as she'd do anything for me and mine.'

That was a masterstroke of emotional manipulation. Jack wanted to shoot to his feet and give her a standing ovation.

'Caro—'

'Uncle Lawrence, I find myself in something of a pickle…'

Without further ado Caro told Lawrence the entire story. By the time she finished the older man had taken off his glasses and was rubbing his eyes.

Caro leaned towards him. 'You *have* to see that I can't let Barbara go to jail.'

He pushed his glasses back to the bridge of his nose. 'Caro, if I take you through to that safety deposit box I will be breaking so many codes of conduct, not to mention laws, that I wouldn't be able to hold my head up in public and—'

'*I* don't actually want to look inside her safety deposit box.'

Jack swung to her. *What on earth…?*

From her bag she pulled out a photograph. 'This is a picture of the missing snuffbox. I don't want to know what else Barbara is storing in the deposit box—that's none of my business. But maybe *you* could check the box to see if that's there.' She pressed the photo into his hand. 'I'm not asking you to remove it—just to see if it's there.'

She stared at her Uncle Lawrence with pleading eyes and Jack held his breath right alongside her.

Lawrence stared at them both for several long moments. 'Do *not* move from those seats.'

Caro crossed her heart. Without another word, Lawrence rose and left.

Caro turned to Jack, sagging in her seat, her hand pressed to her heart. 'I'm so sorry. I can't believe he turned up here today of all days.'

Jack shook his head. 'Not your fault. And this may, in fact, work out better.'

Her shoulders drooped. 'Except now I've involved someone else in my life of crime.'

He meant to say, *Nonsense*. What came out of his mouth instead was, 'You're a godmother?'

A smile suddenly peeked out and he had to catch his breath at the way her face lit up. 'Twice over. To both of Suzie's little girls. Would you like to see a picture?'

'Love to.'

His heart thumped madly when he glanced down at the picture of Caro sitting on a picnic blanket with a toddler in her lap and a baby in her arms. She looked...so happy. His chest twisted. Had he ever made her that happy?

He *wanted* to make her that happy. He wanted—

He blinked when Lawrence came back into the

office. Caro reached across and took the photo from his fingers, flashing it towards Lawrence with an abashed grin before slotting it back into her purse.

They all stared at each other and then Caro shuffled forward to the edge of her chair. If he didn't know better he'd think she'd started to enjoy all this subterfuge and intrigue.

'Well?'

Lawrence slumped down in his chair. 'I didn't find the snuffbox.'

Damn! Jack's hands fisted. Had Barbara managed to dispose of it in that half-day before he'd come on the case? He'd had her tailed ever since. He'd had all the guests at the country house party thoroughly investigated, and had come to the conclusion that Barbara hadn't even taken the snuffbox with her that weekend. Instinct told him she'd gone there to make initial contact with someone. He kept waiting for her to visit one of those guests…or for one of them to turn up at the house in Mayfair. So far, though, there'd been nothing.

'I did, however, find this.'

Jack snapped back to attention when Lawrence placed a locket on the desk in front of Caro.

She stilled, before reaching out to trace it with one finger. 'Mother's locket…'

'That belongs to you.'

Exactly! What on earth was Barbara doing with it? It must be worth a fortune.

'Although I have no real memory of her, all my life I've felt overshadowed by my mother.' She stared at the locket with pursed lips. 'My father set that charity up in her name and then expected me to devote my life to running it. He turned my mother into a kind of saint, and there's not a living, breathing woman who can compete with that. It wouldn't surprise me in the least to find that Barbara has felt overshadowed by the first Mrs Fielding too.' She scooped up the locket with its heavy ornate gold chain and put it in Lawrence's hand. 'Put it back. I have so much. I don't need this.'

Lawrence stared down at the locket, his face grim. 'There are some rather interesting items in that deposit box…'

Caro shook her head. 'Barbara is entitled to her secrets. I have no right to them. I have no desire to pry further than I already have.' She moved to where Lawrence sat and pressed a kiss to his brow. 'I can't thank you enough for all you've done. May I come to dinner some time soon?'

'You know you're welcome any time. Your Auntie Kate would love to see you.'

He rose and kissed both Caro's cheeks. As he did so he held his business card out to Jack behind

Caro's back. Jack pocketed it before Caro could notice the exchange.

'It was nice to meet you, sir.'

'I'm reserving my judgment,' Lawrence said in reply.

Jack and Caro walked back to the car without exchanging a single word. As soon as they reached it, however, Caro started hopping from one foot to the other. Her eyes glittered and her cheeks flushed pink with what he guessed was an excess of adrenaline.

'That was…' She reached out as if to pluck a word from the air.

'A close call,' he finished for her. 'If Lawrence Gardner didn't hold you in such high esteem we'd be toast by now.'

She grabbed his arm, all but dancing. 'Jack, I can't remember the last time I felt so…*alive*!'

'And you call *me* an adrenaline junkie.'

He kept his voice teasing, but all the while he was aware of her grip on his arm and the warm smile dancing across her lips. An ache as big as the Great Barrier Reef opened up inside him. His every molecule screamed at him to kiss her.

'I could get addicted to that.'

Addiction? He stared down at her luscious mouth. Yes, he understood addiction. He thought he might explode into a thousand tiny pieces if he didn't kiss her.

You can't kiss her. You promised.

'Thank you.'

'What for?' he croaked.

'For believing I could pull that off.'

Tenderness rose up through him, warring with his desire—and they entwined, forming something stronger and brighter. 'You were brilliant.' It was nothing less than the truth. 'You saved the day.'

'I can't remember the last time I had to think quickly on my feet like that. For a split second I didn't know whether to lie or to confide in Lawrence.'

'You followed your instincts and they didn't let you down.'

She reached up on tiptoe and kissed his cheek. He bit back a groan.

'I...'

Her voice trailed off at whatever she saw in his face. Her eyes met his and darkened. Her gaze lowered to his lips and her own lips parted ever so slightly—as if she were parched, or as if she couldn't quite catch her breath. Wind roared in his ears. She wanted him. With the same desperate hunger that ravaged him. He'd promised not to kiss her, but...

He moved in closer, traced a finger down the soft flesh of her cheek. Her breath hitched. Her eyes never left his.

'You…' She hiccupped again as his finger moved down the line of her throat. 'You promised,' she whispered.

'I promised not to kiss you,' he murmured. 'I don't recall promising not to touch you. You can tell me to stop any time you want to and I will.'

Her lips parted, but no words emerged.

A surge of something hot and primal pulsed through him. 'And I don't recall *you* promising not to kiss *me*.'

Her breath hitched again. Maintaining eye contact, he took her hand and raised it to his lips, nibbled on the end of her ring finger and then her middle finger, drawing it ever so slightly into the warmth of his mouth.

'You didn't promise you wouldn't kiss me,' he whispered again. 'And I want you to kiss me, Caro. I want that more than I've ever wanted anything in my life.'

A shiver shook through her. He went hard in an instant.

'I didn't promise that I wouldn't put my arms around you…'

Very slowly she shook her head. 'No, you didn't promise that.'

Very slowly he backed up until he was leaning against the car. He drew her towards him to stand between his legs—not quite touching, but their heat swirled and merged and another shiver shook through her.

He kissed the tips of each of the fingers of the hand he still held. 'I didn't promise not to place your arm around my neck…'

He put her hand on his shoulder, snaking an arm about her waist and pulling her closer. The feel of her in his arms was familiar and strange both at the same time. Her other hand slid about his neck too.

'Jack…' she whispered.

He moved his face to within millimetres of hers. 'I didn't promise not to ask you to kiss me…'

'Oh…'

The word was nothing more than a breath and it whispered across his lips, drawing everything inside of him tight. Her hands tightened about his neck.

'I'm not asking, Caro,' he groaned. 'I'm begging. Please kiss me. I—'

She leant forward and pressed her lips to his.

CHAPTER NINE

THE MOMENT HER lips touched his Jack had to fight the torrent of need that roared through him. It took all his strength to let her take the lead and not crush her to him. He didn't want to overwhelm her with his intensity. He didn't want to frighten her with his hunger. He wanted her to remain right here, where she belonged—in his arms.

His hunger was all about *him* and he wanted this kiss to be all about *her*—he wanted to give her everything she needed, everything she craved. He wanted their kiss to tempt, to tease and to tantalise her on every level.

He didn't want the kiss ever to stop. He wanted it to whet her appetite—for him, for *them*. He wanted it to challenge her belief that they couldn't be fixed.

She pressed in closer and a groan broke from him. 'You're killing me.'

She laughed, her breath feathering across his lips. 'And here I was thinking I was kissing you.'

He grazed his teeth across the sensitive skin of her neck, just below her ear, and she melted against him. 'Jack…' His name left her on a whisper, filling him with vigour and a lethal patience.

He kissed a slow path down her throat, revelling in the taste of her and the satin glide of her skin. He moulded her to him—one hand in the small of her back, the other between her shoulderblades. Slipping his lower hand beneath the soft material of her shirt, he lightly raked his fingernails across her bare skin as he kissed his way up the other side of her throat.

She gasped and shivered and pressed herself all the more firmly against him. He wanted to give her so much pleasure it would blot everything else from her mind—the pain he'd caused her, the mistakes they'd made five years ago.

He wanted her filled—body and soul—with the promise of their future. A future he had utter faith in.

He moved his lips back to hers, pressing light kisses at the corners of her mouth, wanting to drive her wild with wanting. Her hands slid up through his hair to hold him still, and his heart pounded until he thought it might burst. She slanted her mouth over his—all open-mouthed heat and wild need—and Jack couldn't contain himself any longer. It was like coming home. It was like being welcomed home.

Fireworks of celebration exploded behind the backs of his eyes. He crushed her to him, wanting the line between where she started and he ended to blur until they became one.

Caro wrapped her arms around Jack's neck and held on for dear life as the maelstrom of desire they'd always ignited in each other rocked through her, lifting her off her feet and hurtling her along with a speed that would have stolen her breath if Jack hadn't already done so. It should frighten her, except she knew Jack would keep her safe. He would never let any harm come to her.

To feel him, to taste him again, alternately soothed and electrified her. It was so familiar, and yet so dark and dangerous. An utter contradiction. Kissing Jack was like every risk she'd ever taken rolled into one—and it was like every warm blanket she'd ever pulled about herself. Kissing Jack was like being flung out of her mind and body at the same time. It was heady and wild.

And it was frightening too—what if she never found herself again? She didn't want to lose herself. Not completely. Not for all time. If she made love with Jack now where would she ever find the strength to be true to herself? How would she be able to resist all that he would ask of her? She would try to become everything he wanted—

needed—and in the process she'd become something neither one of them would recognise.

And then she would have nothing.

Half sobbing, she reefed herself out of his arms. Backing up a couple of steps, she leaned against the car to try and catch her breath. Jack closed his eyes and bent at the waist to draw in great lungfuls of air. She forced her gaze away from him, tried to stamp down on the regrets rising through her, tried to ignore her body's insistent demand for release.

An hour of heaven was not worth another five years of hell.

She started when two arms slammed either side of her on the car, trapping her within their circle. 'You are the most divine woman I have ever met.'

And he was the most divine man she'd ever met—but she wasn't going to say that out loud. She hitched up her chin. 'That could be a sign that you need to get out more.'

He stared down at her, and she didn't know what he saw in her face, but it left her feeling naked.

One corner of his mouth hooked up. 'You never were a pushover.'

Could've fooled her.

'We need to talk, Caro.'

'About the fact we're still attracted to each other?' What was the point of that?

'We could start there.'

She shook her head. 'I can't see there's much we can do about it.'

'Really?' he drawled, cocking a suggestive eyebrow.

She found it hard to stamp down on the laugh that rose through her. In the back of her mind the salsa teacher's voice sounded: *You will flirt!*

'Not going to happen, Jack.'

He raised that eyebrow higher.

She shook her head, but it was harder than it should have been. 'An hour of pleasure is not worth a lifetime of regrets.'

He leaned in closer. 'I can make it last longer than an hour.'

God forgive her, but her breath hitched at the promise lacing his words.

'Do you really think we'd have been able to stop if we'd been at your flat or in my hotel room rather than in a car park?'

She didn't know the answer to that, and she had no intention of finding out. 'I never thought I'd say this, but I'm glad this happened in a public place.'

He reached out and brushed his thumb across her over-sensitised lips. It was all she could do not to moan and touch her tongue to him.

'You still want me.'

'With every atom of my body,' she agreed.

His eyes darkened and his breathing grew shallow at her admission.

'But I am not a mindless body controlled by impulse. I possess a brain, and that brain is telling me not to just walk away from this, Jack, but to run.'

'You're frightened.'

'You should be too! You didn't emerge unscathed the last time we did this.'

He made as if to cradle her cheek, but she snapped upright.

'You're crowding me.'

He immediately dropped his arms and moved back. She paced the length of the car before coming back to stand in front of him.

'We have no future together, and I cannot do some kind of final fling with you. I've worked too hard to get over you to risk undoing all my hard work now.'

He stared at her for a long moment. 'I beg to differ with you on one point, Caro.'

She folded her arms and tapped a foot. 'Really?'

'I believe we *could* have a future together.'

Her arms slackened. Her jaw dropped. 'You *can't* be serious.'

His eyes grew keen and bright. 'I've never been more serious about anything in my life.'

Fear, raw and primal, scrabbled through her, drawing her chest tight.

'What makes you—' he leant down so they were eye to eye '—so certain we *don't* have a future?'

'Our past!' she snapped. He was being ridiculous! Nostalgia was making him sentimental.

'We can learn from the mistakes of our past.'

'Or we could simply repeat them.'

He shook his head. 'I'm smarter now. I know what it is I really want—and that's you.'

No! She wouldn't believe him. She *couldn't*. 'What about children.'

'I don't care if we have children or not.'

How long would that last? 'I don't believe you.' This time she moved in close, invading his personal space. 'I think you want children as much as you ever did.'

His eyes flashed. 'I want you more.'

She stepped back. She wouldn't be able to live with him making that kind of sacrifice.

'Does *nothing* of what I say make any impact on you?' he demanded, his voice ragged.

She swung away and closed her eyes against the pain cramping her chest. 'Jack, for the last five years you've held me solely responsible for the breakdown of our marriage. In the last eight days you've been confronted with your own culpability. I understand your sense of guilt, I understand your desire to make amends and to try and put things right, but…' She turned, gripping the tops of her arms tightly. 'We cannot be put to rights. There's no longer any *"we"* that can be salvaged.'

Her words seemed to beat at him like blows and each of them left her feeling bruised and shaken.

He seized her by the shoulders, his face pale though his eyes blazed. 'I love you, Caro. Doesn't that mean anything to you?'

Yearning yawned through her. To have…

No!

She hardened her heart and shook her head. 'I don't wish to be cruel, Jack, but no, I'm afraid it doesn't.'

Turning grey, he let her go, his shoulders slumping as if she'd just run him through with a sword. She had to bite her lip to stifle the cry that rose up through her.

Why had he ever come back to London?

Why hadn't he simply sent the divorce papers through the post?

She'd rather he'd continued to blame her—hate her—than put him through this kind of emotional torment.

She had to leave before she did something stupid, like hurl herself into his arms and say sorry, tell him she loved him too. Love wasn't enough. It never had been. It was better they face that now than another twelve months down the track.

She pulled herself up to her full height. 'I'll see myself home.'

He stiffened. 'Get in the car, Caro. I will take you home.'

Her hands clenched. 'I am not a child who can be ordered about or cajoled. I have a free will, which I'm choosing to assert now. I would much prefer to see myself home.' She tried to pull in a steadying breath. 'But thank you for the offer.'

He stared at her, shoved his hands in his pockets. 'Right.'

She moistened her lips. 'I think it'd be for the best if we didn't see each other again.'

His head jerked up. 'The snuffbox—'

'Is lost forever, I expect.'

'I haven't given up hope.'

She had.

'At nine o'clock on Friday morning—' the day after tomorrow '—I'll be informing my boss that I've lost the snuffbox and I will tender my resignation.'

The pulse in his jaw jumped, but he didn't say a word.

'I'd like you to send me a bill for your time and expenses, though I suspect you won't.'

'You suspect right.'

'I'll sign the divorce papers and have them sent to your lawyer.'

She couldn't say any more. Her throat ached too much from saying the word *divorce*—it lodged there like a block of solid wood, its hard edges pressing into her with such ferocity it made her vision blur.

She spun away and made for the exit. 'Good-bye, Jack.'

The letters on the car park exit sign blurred, but she kept her focus trained on their neon glow rather than the throb at her temples or the pain pressing down on her chest. It took all her strength to remain upright and to place one foot in front of the other.

This was for the best. She could never trust Jack again. She could never be certain that the next time she failed to measure up to his expectations he wouldn't just walk away again. And she wouldn't be able to bear that.

She hadn't made him happy five years ago. Oh, they'd had great sex—there was no denying that—but a solid marriage needed stronger glue than great sex. She and Jack…they didn't have that glue.

The sunshine made her blink when she finally arrived outside. She scowled at it. How dared the day be so…*summery*?

She caught the tube home. *Please, please, please, don't be one of those people who cry on the train.* She couldn't bear the mortification of that.

She might not be able to turn the pain off, but she could try and corral her thoughts. She recited the alphabet silently until she reached her stop. On wooden legs, she turned in at Jean-Pierre's bakery.

He spun with a smile that faded when he took in her expression. *'Ma cherie.'* He shook his head. 'Not a good day?'

'Dreadful, dreadful day,' she agreed tonelessly. 'The worst.' She gestured to his counter full of cakes. 'I'm looking for something that will make me feel better.'

Sugar wasn't the answer. They both knew that. But she blessed his tact in remaining silent on the subject. He packed her up an assortment. She trudged upstairs to her flat and sat at the table. She stared at the cakes for several long minutes—a chocolate éclair, a strawberry tart, a vanilla slice and a tiny lemon meringue pie.

She couldn't dredge up the slightest enthusiasm for a single one of them.

The longer she stared at them the more her eyes stung. A lump lodged in her throat. Shaking her head, she lifted the chocolate éclair to her lips and bit into it. She chewed and with a superhuman effort swallowed. She set the éclair back down. Its dark brown icing gleamed the exact same colour as Jack's hair—

Slamming a halt to those thoughts, she picked up the lemon meringue pie, bit into it, chewed and swallowed. She did the same with the strawberry tart and then the vanilla slice. With each bite the lump in her throat subsided. It lodged in her chest instead, where it became a hard, bitter ache.

She stared at the delicacies, each with a dainty bite taken out of them, and pushed the cake box away to rest her head on her hands.

Jack started when he realised darkness had begun creeping across the floor of his hotel room. He barely remembered returning here earlier in the afternoon, but the stiffness in his muscles told him he'd been sitting in this chair for hours.

He glanced across to the window. The grey twilight on the other side of the glass complemented the greyness stretching through him.

He closed his eyes. Every fibre of his being ached to go and find Caro and change her mind—to fight harder for her—but...

He rested his head in his hands. The look on her face when he'd told her he loved her... He'd wanted to see joy, hope, delight. He'd wanted her to throw her arms around his neck and tell him she loved him too.

Instead...

He dropped his head back to the headrest of his chair. Instead she'd stared at him with a kind of stricken horror that had made his heart shrivel.

He understood now how out of character it had been for Caro to fall in love with him so quickly six and a half years ago. How out of character it had been for her to marry him after knowing him for only four months. By nature Caro was a careful person, but she'd loved him back then. She'd trusted him completely, and when he'd left he'd not only broken her heart, he'd broken faith with her, he'd made her doubt her own judgment.

He should have fought for her five years ago!

He'd misinterpreted her reserve as meaning she didn't love him. Instead of challenging her, though, he'd run away. *Like a coward.*

He'd blown it. He'd get no second chance with her. She'd never let him close again, regardless of the promises he made her.

What promises have you made? What exactly have you offered her?

He frowned at the gathering darkness. With a curse, he leapt to his feet and switched on the lamp before reaching for his laptop. There were no promises he could make that Caro would believe, but he had promised to do all he could to retrieve that damn snuffbox. That was one thing he *could* do for her.

Settling earphones over his head, he tuned in to the listening devices he'd placed in the house in Mayfair earlier in the week. *Give me something!*

Two hours later he pulled the earphones from his head and flung them to the desk.

Eureka!

He backed up the files in three different locations, emailed them to each of his email accounts, burnt them to a CD and loaded them on to a thumb drive as a final precaution. Next he researched the government's National Archive. Forty minutes later he tossed both the CD and the thumb drive into his satchel. Throwing the bag over his shoulder, he set off on foot for Mayfair.

'Mr Jack,' Paul boomed when he opened the door. 'It's very good to see you.'

That wasn't what the treacherous snake in the grass would be saying in ten minutes' time.

'Jack?' Barbara appeared in the doorway of the drawing room. 'Is Caro with you?'

'No.'

He might have misjudged Barbara—just as Caro had said—but she was still as treacherous as Paul in her own way. Though at least now he understood her.

Barbara moved more fully into the foyer, a frown marring the china doll perfection of her face. 'Is everything all right, darling? Is Caro all right?'

'Caro is fine, as far as I know.' And he meant to keep it that way. 'But everything is far from all right. I need the two of you to listen to something. Do you have a CD player?'

Barbara swept an arm towards the drawing room

and directed him across to the far wall, where a stereo system perched on an antique credenza.

'Don't go, Paul,' Jack added, not turning around but sensing the older man's intention to withdraw. 'I want you to hear this too.'

He put the disc into the player, surreptitiously retrieving one of his listening devices as he did so. He'd retrieve them all before he left this evening. He pressed the play button.

'You might want to sit,' he said, gesturing to the sofas.

Barbara and Paul both remained standing.

'This necklace didn't come from Roland, Paul, and we both know it.'

As her voice emerged from the speakers, Barbara sank down into the nearest chair with a gasp, her hand fluttering up to her throat.

'There's only one person who could possibly be responsible for this, and that's Caro.'

A short pause followed, and then Paul's voice emerged from the speakers. *'Yes.'*

Jack could almost see the older man's nod as he agreed with Barbara.

'I don't want to do this any more, Paul. I want Caro to know the truth.'

'We can't! We promised her father! And there's your mother to think of. You could never afford her medical bills on your own.'

Jack reached over and switched the CD player

off. 'I could let it keep running, but we all know what it says.'

Barbara lifted her head and swallowed. 'I'm glad the truth will come out now.'

And yet only a couple of hours ago she'd submitted to Paul's bullying.

'Are you *utterly* faithless?' Paul shot at her.

His words were angry, but everything about him had slumped, as if he were caving in on himself.

'Faithless?' Jack found himself shouting. 'What about the faith you should've been keeping with Caro? She loves the two of you! She considers you her family. And this is how you treat her?'

Barbara wasn't a woman easily given to tears, but she looked close to them now. He sensed her regret was genuine. And, considering the bribery Roland had used to sway her, he could almost forgive her. *Almost.*

He shoved his shoulders back. 'Shall I share the conclusions I've come to?'

Barbara spread her hands in a *please continue* gesture. Paul said nothing, but his back had bowed and he'd lost his colour.

'Sit, Paul,' Jack ordered.

The other man's head lifted. 'I'm the butler, Mr Jack. The butler doesn't—'

'Can it! You lost all rights to butler etiquette the moment you started this nasty little game.'

Without another word, Paul sat. Jack stared at them both, trying to swallow back the fury coursing through him.

'Before he died, Caro's father made the two of you promise to sabotage Caro's job at Richardson's in an attempt to have her fired—so you could force her hand and have her finally take over the administration of that damn trust.'

Barbara hesitated, and then nodded. 'He thought that by making her the sole beneficiary of his will it would soften her attitude towards both him *and* the trust.'

'And of course the two of *you* were to do everything you could to encourage that softening?'

She winced and nodded.

'I also know that if you succeeded, you were both to be rewarded.'

Barbara's head came up.

'I suspect your mother's hospital bills and her care were to be guaranteed if you succeeded.' He named the medical facility where Barbara's mother resided. 'I know the kind of care she needs, and I know how much that costs.'

She shot to her feet, visibly shaken. 'How do you know about that?'

'I'm a private investigator. I'm trained to follow a lead.'

He'd found out Barbara's mother's name and had tracked her to a private medical clinic in Northumberland. A phone call had confirmed that she had a severe dissociative personality disorder and needed round-the-clock psychological monitoring. She was receiving the very best of care. The fees, however, were astronomical.

Barbara sat again, brushing her hand across her eyes. 'I can't even visit her. It upsets her too much. Making sure she gets the best of care is the one thing I *can* do.'

He couldn't imagine how difficult that must be. 'I'm sorry about your mother, Barbara.'

'Thank you.'

'Roland blackmailed you?'

She glanced up and gave a strained shrug. 'In a way, I suppose. But you see I *did* love him. Ours wasn't a wild, romantic relationship, but... I wanted him to be happy. It didn't really seem too much to ask of Caro, to administer that wretched trust, but...'

'But?'

She lifted her head. 'But, regardless of what the rest of us think or want, Caro has a right to make her own decisions in respect to her life.'

His heart thumped. 'I couldn't agree more.' He just wished she'd made the decision to include *him* in her life. Pushing that thought aside, he turned to Paul. 'What I don't understand is why *you'd* agree to Roland's games. I thought you cared about Caro?'

'I do!'

Nobody spoke for several long moments.

'He just loved Caro's mother more,' Barbara finally said, breaking the silence that had descended.

Jack fell into a seat then too. Paul? In love with Caro's mother?

'I went too far.' Paul rested his head in his hands. 'What are you going to do, Mr Jack?' he asked.

If Caro didn't care about these two so much he'd throw them to the wolves. But she *did* care about them.

It occurred to him then that his idea of family had been utterly unrealistic—a complete fantasy. Family, it appeared, was about accepting others' foibles and eccentricities. It was about taking into account and appreciating their weaknesses as much as their strengths.

He leaned towards the other two. 'Okay, listen carefully. This is what we're going to do…'

Caro was brushing her teeth on Friday morning when Jack's knock sounded on her door.

She knew it was Jack. She refused to contemplate too closely *how* she knew that, though.

She rinsed her mouth and considered not answering.

'Caro? I have the snuffbox.'

His voice penetrated the thick wood of her door. She stared at it, and then flew across to fling it open. 'If you're teasing me, Jack, I'll—'

He held out the snuffbox, and for a moment all she could do was stare at it.

'Oh!'

She could barely believe it. Maybe...maybe disaster could be averted after all.

With fingers that trembled she took it from him, hardly daring to believe this was the very same snuffbox she'd lost. She took Jack's arm and pulled him into the flat, and then ran to get her eyeglass. She examined it in minute detail.

'What are you doing?'

'Making sure it's authentic and not a replica.'

'Well...?' he asked when she set the eyeglass to the table.

She wanted to dance on the spot. 'It's the very same snuffbox I lost last week.'

She wanted to hug him, but remembered what had happened the last time she'd let her elation overcome her reserve. She pressed a hand to her chest to try and calm the pounding of her heart.

'You've saved the day—just as you promised you would. How? How did you do it?'

He shuffled his feet and darted a glance towards the kitchen. 'Is that coffee I smell?'

She suddenly realised he was wearing the same clothes she'd last seen him in, and that he needed a shave. She padded into the kitchen and poured them a mug of coffee each. She set his mug to the table.

'Have a seat.'

With a groan, he unhooked his satchel from his shoulder and dropped it to the floor, before planting himself in a chair and bringing the mug to his lips. 'Thank you.'

She frowned at him. 'Have you had any sleep in the last two days?'

He made an impatient movement with his hand. 'It's no matter. I can sleep on the plane.'

He was returning to Australia *today*? An ache started up inside her.

It's for the best.

Except the misery he was trying to hide beat at her like a living, breathing thing.

She sipped coffee in an attempt to fortify herself. 'How did you find the snuffbox? Who had it?'

'It was all a comedy of errors, believe it or not, and frankly you needn't have hired me in the first place.'

She frowned. 'What are you talking about?'

He eyed her over the rim of his mug. 'You have an army of cleaners coming in to the Mayfair house twice a week, yes?'

'Yes.'

'It appears that when Barbara made her midnight raid on the safe she dropped the snuffbox on the stairs.'

So why hadn't she or Paul found it?

'The next day the maid dusting the staircase found it and placed it in the sideboard in the dining room. She thought it was some kind of fancy spice pot, or something along those lines.'

'And therefore thought it belonged with the dining ware?'

'Of course she forgot to mention to anyone what she'd done.'

She gaped at him. 'So it was never Barbara? Oh, I should burn in brimstone forever for thinking such a shocking thing of her!'

His lips pressed together in a thin tight line.

'It's such a simple explanation! But…how did you find all of this out?'

'I rang the cleaning service you use, spoke to the woman in charge and asked her to check with the staff.'

Amazingly simple—and yet…

'I'd never have thought of that. I did right in hiring you, Jack.' She swallowed. 'You've saved the day and I can't thank you enough.'

'I'm glad I could help.'

He rose and her heart started to burn.

'It's time I was going.' He barely looked at her. 'Goodbye, Caro.'

She couldn't make her legs work to walk him

to the door. It closed behind him and she had to blink hard for several moments and concentrate on her breathing.

Last night's cake box still sat on the table. Seizing it, she strode into the kitchen and tossed it into the bin. Sugar wasn't the answer. Nothing but time would ease the pain scoring through her now.

She limped back to the table and picked up the snuffbox, clasped it to her chest. 'Thank you, Jack,' she whispered to the silent room. 'Thank you.'

She went to turn away—it was time for her to dress for work—when something black and silver under the table caught her attention. She reached down and picked it up. A CD. Had she dropped it? Or had Jack?

It wasn't labelled. With a shrug, she slotted it into her CD player. If it belonged to Jack she'd post it to him in Australia. She glanced at the case again, but it gave no clue.

And then two voices sounded from the speakers and her mug froze halfway to her mouth.

'I don't want to do this any more, Paul. I want Caro to know the truth.'

'We can't! We promised her father!'

CHAPTER TEN

CARO PLANTED HERSELF in a chair and listened to the CD twice more.

'So…' She drummed her fingers against the table. 'The maid never put it in the sideboard after all…' She pressed her fingers to her temples. Paul and Barbara had joined forces to take the snuff-box *together*. She stared up at the ceiling. 'I didn't even think they *liked* each other.'

Actually, the recording didn't change her mind in that regard. Obviously her father had compelled them to sabotage her career. No doubt in the hope that she'd take over that damn trust. What did he have on them? Why would they agree to do such a thing to her? She'd thought they cared about her!

She shot to her feet to pace about the room. Why had Jack lied? Why hadn't he told her the truth? For a moment she wanted to throw things at the walls and shout *No one can be trusted. No one!*

She passed a hand across her eyes. Except that would be histrionic—not to mention an unwarrantable generalisation—and she didn't do histrionics.

With the most unladylike curse she knew, she spun away to storm into her bedroom. She'd just had over a week's leave. The least she could do was get her butt over to Fredrick Soames's house in Knightsbridge and sell him this rotten snuffbox.

Freddie set the snuffbox to his desk and pursed his lips. 'It's a pretty piece, I grant you.'

'It *is* pretty.' Caro crossed her legs. 'But…?'

'The price is rather steep.'

'That's nonsense, Freddie, and you know it.' She'd known the Honourable Frederick Robert Arthur Soames for her entire life. Her father and his father had both been at Eton together.

He pulled a notepad towards him. 'I'd be prepared to pay…' He jotted down an amount, turned the pad around and pushed it across towards her.

The sum was significantly lower than the price she'd just quoted him.

Freddie loved to play games. And he really loved a bargain.

Caro crossed out the amount and jotted down a significantly higher figure. 'In all conscience I cannot allow my client to accept an amount lower than that. If you choose to pass at that price then we'll take our chances at auction.'

His face dropped comically. 'But…but that's the original asking price.'

She smiled. After all the trouble this snuffbox had caused, she had every intention of getting the best price possible for it.

'Listen, Caro, I know it's your job to do the best for your client, but we've known each other for a long time and—'

'Don't you dare say another word, Freddie Soames. We may have known each other forever, and we may indeed be friends, but I am *not* cutting you a deal on this snuffbox. You should know better than to even ask.'

His shrug was completely without rancour. 'You can't blame a guy for trying. You have a hard-nosed reputation in the industry.' He said it in such an admiring tone that she had to laugh. 'It's so at odds with your personality outside of work that I just…wanted to try my luck,' he finished with a grin.

At odds with her…? That made her grow sober again. Was that why Paul and Barbara had thought they could walk all over her? Was that why…? She gulped. Was that why Jack had left her five years ago?

If she brought the same backbone and strength of purpose to her personal relationships as she did to her work, would it make a difference? If she'd put her foot down and stated, *This is what I expect*

*from all of you—honesty, respect and acceptance.
And if you can't promise me that then...then...*

Jack had said he could give her all of those things.

But she hadn't believed him.

Out of nowhere her heart started to thump.

'Caro, are you okay?'

She started, and shot Freddie a smile. 'I'm simply tickety-boo, Freddie.'

It occurred to her that now she had the snuffbox back in her keeping she was curiously reluctant to let it go.

Time to force Freddie's hand. 'Richardson's has given you first option on this beautiful example of a seventeenth-century snuffbox, but you must understand that interest in these items is always high. I'm going to count to three. You have until then either to accept at the asking price—' she touched a finger to the notepad '—or to decline.'

'No need to count, Caro.' He leaned back, fingers clasped behind his head. 'I'm going to chance my luck when it goes to auction.'

She laughed at the light of competition that sparkled from his eyes. As she'd known it would. '*If* it makes it to auction, Freddie. Don't count your chickens.'

She wrapped the snuffbox in a soft cloth, placed it into a protective box and slipped it into her purse. 'It was lovely to see you.' She shook his hand and left.

She stood on his doorstep for a moment. Freddie Soames lived in Knightsbridge...maybe that was why Lawrence Gardner popped into her mind. She glanced at her watch. The interview with Freddie hadn't taken nearly as long as she'd thought it would. On impulse, she dialled Lawrence's number.

'I wonder if you have a moment or two to spare for me?' she said after their greetings.

'Absolutely, my dear girl. I'm in the Knightsbridge branch today.'

'I'm about two minutes away.'

'So this is the offending item that caused all the trouble.' Lawrence handed the snuffbox back to her. 'I'm very pleased you recovered it.'

'Oh, yes, I am too.' She told him the story Jack had given her.

His gaze slid away. 'All's well that ends well, then.'

She folded her arms. 'You don't believe that story any more than I do. I *know* Paul and Barbara were behind the snuffbox's disappearance... at my father's behest.'

'Ah...'

'Has Jack been to see you since our...uh... unscheduled meeting at the bank on Wednesday?'

He hesitated and then nodded. 'I believe that boy has your best interests at heart, though, Caro.'

She pulled in a breath and nodded. 'I do too.'

'Right, well… Jack came to see me this morning. He wanted a couple of bank cheques drawn up.'

She listened closely to all he had to tell her and her heart started to burn. 'Father blackmailed Barbara and…and threatened to cut off the funds for her mother's care? That's…diabolical!'

Lawrence winced.

'Why didn't she come to me? She had to know that I'd take care of it.'

She suddenly recalled Barbara's words from the night they'd spent in Kent. *You've always been a funny little thing... It can be very difficult to get a handle on how you truly feel.* Maybe…maybe Barbara *hadn't* known.

She cursed her own reserve. And Barbara's.

'I can't imagine, though, why *Paul* would agree to do such a thing.' Lawrence sighed. 'He dotes on you.'

'Oh, that's easy.' She rubbed a hand across her chest. 'He was in love with my mother. I believe she's the only woman he's ever loved.'

'Good God!'

She smiled at the appalled expression on Lawrence's face. 'No, no—I don't believe for a single moment that there was anything between them other than mutual respect and friendship.'

'Thank God!' He sagged back in his chair. 'But if you're right it would explain why he'd be so set on you taking over management of the trust.'

'I can't believe I never saw it before now, but all my life he's tried to gently guide me towards it. I thought he was simply trying to be conciliatory—to improve matters between Father and me.'

A sense of betrayal niggled at the edges of her consciousness, but she pushed it away. It would be easy to retreat behind a sense of outrage and betrayal, but what would that achieve? The last time she'd done that it had led to five years of misery.

'So Jack's taken it upon himself to try and put this all to rights?'

Lawrence spread his hands and nodded. 'What are you going to do? Is there anything I can do to help?'

She leaned across his desk to clasp his hand. 'You have already done so much and I will be eternally grateful.' She pulled in a breath. '*I'm* going to make things right—that's what I'm going to do. Although I could use some help with a couple of practical matters.'

He straightened. 'I'm a practical man. Fire away.'

Three hours later Caro let herself into the house in Mayfair. A voice emerging from the room to her left informed her that Paul, at least, was in.

She moved across to the doorway of her father's study and her heart hammered up into her throat, before settling back to bang and crash in her chest.

Jack!

Jack was here. He hadn't left for Australia yet. Somewhere inside her she started to salsa.

The internal twirling faltered when she remembered that flights to Australia didn't usually depart Heathrow until the evening. Her heart nose-dived to her toes. Jack's flight was probably six or seven hours away yet. He still had plenty of time to make it.

Unless she managed to change his mind.

She moistened suddenly dry lips. Her happiness was in her own hands. All she had to do was reach out and take what she wanted.

If she dared.

'Caro, darling!' Barbara shot to her feet, a look of dismay settling over her features. 'Darling, I…' She fell back into her chair, her words trailing off as if she had no idea what to say.

Caro didn't blame her. Squaring her shoulders, she strode up to the desk. 'I'd like to take the floor for a moment, if you don't mind,' she said to Jack and Paul.

She pointed to the two chairs on either side of Barbara, and after a moment's hesitation the two men moved to them.

Paul could barely meet her eye.

Jack stared at her with such undisguised hunger it made her blood rush in her ears, but his gaze snapped away when he realised she'd surveyed him and he shuffled the papers he held in his hands instead. An ache swelled through her.

She slid up to sit on the desk, but had to swallow a couple of times before she could risk speaking. Her voice jammed in her chest again when Jack darted a glance of frank appreciation at her legs.

That sealed it. She knew *exactly* what she was going to do.

But first...

She reached into her purse and pulled out the CD. 'I believe this belongs to you, Jack.'

Barbara closed her eyes. Paul paled.

Jack's eyes darkened as he took it from her outstretched hand.

'It must've fallen from your bag when you visited me earlier. You really should learn to fasten the latches on that thing.'

She could see his mind flicking back to this morning. 'I pulled the snuffbox from it and...'

'And then dropped said bag to the floor when you had your coffee.'

'Without fastening it again.' The pulse in his jaw pounded. He raised the CD slightly. 'Did you listen to it?'

'Oh, yes.'

All three of them winced.

She reached out and plucked the documents Jack held from his other hand. Cheques. One made out to the facility where Barbara's mother resided and the other made out to her mother's trust. Both for huge sums. *Oh, Jack! This isn't your mess to clean up.* Shaking her head, Caro tore the cheques into sixteen fragments apiece.

Barbara pressed the heel of her hand to her mouth to stifle a sob.

'Okay, so here's the deal,' Caro continued calmly, dumping the scraps of paper on the desk behind her. She opened her folder and brought out the first in a series of documents. 'Barbara, this paperwork here, as you'll see, is a contract between the facility where your mother is kept and me. It ensures that your mother's care is guaranteed. I do wish you'd trusted me to take care of this in the first place.'

God, she was magnificent.

Jack stared at Caro and his skin tingled as a rush of warmth shot through him. He hadn't been sure how she'd deal with the truth of all this, but he could see now that he should have trusted her with it. She was all class.

'Oh, I…' Barbara had to wipe her fingers beneath her eyes, to mop up the tears that had started to fall.

'I understand that my…reserve has made you

unsure of me. I am sorry for that. I also understand that your loyalty must've felt torn between my father and me as well.'

The other woman lifted her chin. 'The fact of the matter is I did marry your father for his money, darling. I wanted my mother taken care of properly.'

Caro nodded. 'And in return for that my father received a wonderful wife who always went the extra mile for him. I still think he received the better part of that deal. I want you to know that I've had several million pounds transferred into your account—'

'That is absolutely unnecessary! I don't—'

'Humour me, Barbara. I've also had the deeds to the villa in Spain transferred into your name.'

Barbara swallowed. 'You'd like me to move out?' She nodded. 'Of course you do—'

'Absolutely not! I just know how much you love that villa. You and Father honeymooned there.'

'Oh, but, Caro darling, it's all too much.'

'Nonsense.' Caro turned from Barbara to Paul. 'Now, Paul.'

Jack leaned back, folding his arms and enjoying the show.

'It's occurred to me that if my mother's trust means so much to you then *you* are probably the perfect person to manage it. This document here—' she held up a sheaf of papers '—names you as chairman of the trust's board.'

'Miss Caroline, I—'

'Caro!' she ordered.

Paul swallowed. 'Caro, I...I don't know what to say.'

'Say you'll accept the position and that you'll do your best to execute the duties of the post.'

'You have my word,' he croaked, falling back into his seat.

'I've also arranged for a pension for you. Something my father should've taken care of before he died. It will be in addition to the salary you draw from administering the trust.'

The older man's head shot up. 'I won't be drawing a salary from the trust! It will be an honour to administer it.'

Caro didn't look the least surprised by this avowal. Jack would bet she'd factored that in and had made sure that his pension was very liberal.

'Good grief, Caro! I can't accept this,' he said when she handed him the paperwork outlining the details of the pension. 'This is far too generous.'

'You've earned it. You gave my father sterling service for over thirty years. Besides, I can afford it...and it's what I want.'

Caro drew in a deep breath, and such a roar of longing spiked through Jack, his hand clenched about the seat of his chair to keep him there.

'Now, I want you both to know that these things I've set in motion today are set in stone. They cannot be changed. I cannot revoke or undo what I've just promised you. You are both free to simply walk away from me now, without the fear of any reprisals.'

The room went so still that all Jack could hear was the tick of the grandfather clock out in the entrance hall.

Caro pressed her hands together. 'So now it's time for me to cast aside my wretched reserve and for us to speak plainly with each other. Barbara and Paul—I consider the two of you my family.'

Jack's heart burned that she hadn't included *him* in that number.

'I care about the two of you a great deal. I was hoping my affection was returned.'

'It *is*, darling!'

'I love you like my own daughter!'

'But that didn't stop either of you from trying to sabotage my happiness. If the two of you really care about me then what I demand from you is respect, loyalty and acceptance for who I am. If you can't give me that, then we need to go our separate ways.'

Paul shot to his feet. 'You will have it to my dying day,' he vowed.

'Yes, darling, you have *my* word too.'

Caro's smile was sudden, sweet and utterly enchanting. 'Then we can continue on as we've been doing. I mean to give up my flat and we can all live here in this ridiculous house like the mismatched dysfunctional family that we are.'

Barbara stood in swift elegant motion and pulled Caro from the desk to fold her in a hug. 'Darling, that sounds marvellous.'

Paul waited beside them, impatiently moving from foot to foot, until he had a chance to engulf Caro in a bear hug. 'Splendid! Splendid!'

With a heart that throbbed Jack slipped the strap of his satchel over his shoulder, stood and turned towards the door.

'Where do you think you're going?' Caro called after him, before he'd had the chance to take two steps.

He pulled in a breath, but didn't turn. 'I have a plane to catch.'

'In what—six hours?'

Acid burned his stomach at the thought of flying away from her. He met her gaze briefly. 'I have to be at the airport in four hours' time and…and there are things I need to do before then.'

Number one on that list was: save face and maintain whatever pride he could.

'I was hoping… Please, Jack, could you spare me ten more minutes?'

He should say no. He should toss a casual *sa-*

yonara over his shoulder and walk away from her with a jaunty stride.

Casual? Jaunty? *Impossible.*

Saying no to Caro? Also impossible.

His shoulders slumped. His satchel slid to the floor.

'Sure. What's ten minutes?'

But they both knew what havoc ten minutes could wreak. Six and a half years ago on a reckless impulse he'd asked her to marry him. On impulse she'd said yes. It had taken less than a minute for them to promise to build a life together.

Five years ago, when he'd thought she meant to abort their baby, it had taken him ten minutes to pack his bags and walk away.

When he'd told her he loved her yesterday, it had taken less than a minute for her to shatter his hopes.

What was ten minutes? It could be the most hellish time of his life, that was what.

Or the most heavenly.

He pushed that thought away. He could harbour no hopes.

He snapped back to himself to find Barbara slipping her arm through Paul's and leading him from the room, murmuring something about tea and cake.

He forced his gaze to Caro's. 'You want to take

me to task for keeping the truth about the snuff-box from you?'

She shook her head, her smile spearing into the centre of him. 'It was kind of you to want to protect me from the truth, even if it *was* misguided. It was even kinder of you to offer such large amounts of money to both Barbara and Paul in an attempt to make things right.'

He'd hoped by buying their gratitude it would help offset some of the damage Caro's father had caused.

'If it's not that, what *do* you want to talk to me about?'

Her gaze dropped to her hands and she looked so suddenly uncertain that he took a step towards her. She glanced up and then away again. Finally she reached into her purse and pulled a wrapped object from it. He knew immediately what it was—the snuffbox.

She unwrapped it, placed it on her palm and stared at it for a long moment. 'I bought this earlier today.'

She what? 'You mean to tell me that blasted Soames bloke didn't want it after all?'

'Oh, he wanted it all right.'

Her laugh washed over him and it was all he could do not to close his eyes and memorise it—to help him through tomorrow...and all the days after that.

'But he decided to play games instead—hoping for a lower price—and I found I didn't want to part with it. Regardless of the price offered.'

She held it out to him. 'Jack, I'd like you to have it.'

His jaw dropped. 'That's absolutely not necessary. I told you I didn't require payment, and—'

'It's not payment. I know enough not to challenge you on that. This is a gift. A…a symbol.'

He snapped his mouth shut. He found himself breathing hard, as if he'd just completed the obstacle course at his old police training college. 'A symbol of what?'

She placed the snuffbox in his hand and backed up again, to lean against the edge of the desk. She pushed her bangle up her arm as far as it would go and twisted it.

'I've only just admitted this to myself, but…my heart was lost in the same way that this snuffbox was lost. You found the latter and somehow that helped me to find the former.'

His heart pounded a tattoo against his ribs. He was too afraid to hope. Caro didn't like risks. She avoided them where possible. It would be folly to think she'd risk her heart on him a second time.

'I'm not precisely sure what that means.'

She bit her lip and then looked him full in the face. Her uncertainty almost undid him.

'I never ask for what I want. I'm not sure why

that's the case. Habit, I suppose. What I wanted never mattered much to my father, so I guess I thought what I wanted wouldn't matter much to anyone else either.'

'It matters to me,' he said, moving a step closer. 'Caro, are you saying that you want…*me*? That you want to give our marriage a second chance?'

Her eyes suddenly flashed. '*I* want to be the one to state what I want, Jack. I don't want to leave it up to you. I don't want to leave it up to anyone! I don't want to place people in a position where they have to guess at what I want. I want to overcome this hateful reticence of mine and say exactly what I mean—at least around you, Barbara and Paul.'

She'd just put him in the same category as the rest of her family and his heart all but stopped. It took a moment for him to catch his breath.

'What *do* you want, Caro?'

She met his gaze. 'I want *you*, Jack. I want to spend my life with you. I love you.'

He couldn't contain himself a moment longer. He closed the distance between them and hauled her into his arms. 'You know I'm never going to be able to let you go again, don't you?'

Her eyes throbbed into his. 'I like the sound of that. I also very much want you to kiss me.'

He stared at her infinitely kissable mouth and something in his chest shifted.

'You don't need to ask twice.'

He lowered his mouth towards hers and a fraction of a second before their lips met she smiled, as if she suddenly believed that she could have everything she asked for.

Her hope and delight bathed him in a warmth he'd forgotten that he needed. Cradling her face in his hands, he kissed her. Slowly. Thoroughly. Sweetly.

Her hands slid up either side of his neck and she pressed herself to him, kissing him back with the same thoroughness, the same passion and tenderness, and with the same intent to reassure and pour balm on old wounds.

He savoured every moment, something inside him filling up and easing. Then, in a flash and a touch of tongues, the kiss changed to become hungry, hot and demanding. Jack gave himself up to the heady abandon and the flying freedom of it.

He didn't know how long the kiss lasted, but when they finally eased away from each other it seemed as if the very quality of the light in the room had changed—as if a brand new day had dawned.

Caro touched her tongue to her lips, which did nothing to quieten the hunger roaring through him.

'Wow…' she breathed.

A grin stretched through him. 'You should ask for what you want more often.'

Her eyes danced. 'I mean to.' She reached up to touch his face. 'Jack, I promise to be more open and upfront with you. I know that my reserve played a big role in our troubles five years ago.'

He took her hand, kissed her fingertips. 'We can put that all behind us now. It's in the past.'

She shook her head. 'It's only in the past if we've learned from the mistakes we made back then.'

Ah.

She bit her lip. 'Jack, can you promise me honesty from now on?'

He recalled the promise she'd extracted from Barbara and Paul. 'I can promise you honesty, loyalty and acceptance.'

She smiled. 'I never doubted the second and third of those for a moment. But your urge to protect me…'

He pulled in a breath, knowing he couldn't give this promise lightly. Finally he nodded. 'I promise you honesty, Caro. Even if it's hard for me to say and hard for you to hear.'

'Thank you.'

'You promise me the same?'

'I do,' she said, without hesitation.

She bit her lip again, and while her eyes didn't exactly cloud over the light in them dimmed a fraction.

'What?' he demanded, immediately alert.

'I understand your desire for children and a family, Jack, but hundreds and thousands of couples work it out—negotiate it somehow—so I'm sure we can too, and—'

He touched a finger to her lips, halting her rush of words. 'I've been thinking about this a lot, and I think I've found a solution.'

Her eyes narrowed. 'I don't want you making any unnecessary sacrifices.'

'I don't want you doing that either.'

'Okay...'

She drew the word out and it made him smile. 'If you're not totally against the idea of having children—'

'Oh, I'm not. Not now. Being exposed to Suzie's two—being their godmother—has made me realise that I'll never become the kind of remote parent my father was.'

He stared at her. 'I wish you'd told me that was what you were afraid of five years ago.' He didn't want to make the same mistakes ever again where this woman was concerned. He pushed a strand of hair back behind her ear. 'Why didn't you ever tell me?'

One of her shoulders lifted. 'I didn't want you to laugh at me.'

'I would never laugh at you.'

'And I didn't want my fear dismissed as nonsense.'

He nodded slowly. 'The fear isn't nonsense, but the idea that you could be anything less than a loving mother seems crazy to me,' he admitted.

'I'm confident enough in myself now to see the difference.'

He touched the backs of his fingers to her cheek. 'We married too soon, didn't we?'

Five years ago he'd wanted all his dreams to come true then and there.

She caught his hand in hers and kissed it. 'I understand we needed a trial by fire to cement what was really important. I only wish it hadn't take us five years to get through it.'

He wanted to wipe the sadness and the remembered pain from her eyes. 'I promise to never walk away from you the way I did five years ago. I should've stayed and fought for you back then. I will always fight for you, Caro.'

The brilliance of her smile almost blindsided him. 'I think I'm going to have to ask you to kiss me again.'

He laughed. 'How does this sound? When you're ready, we can start a family…and if you want to return to work then that's what you'll do, and I can be the stay-at-home parent.'

Her eyes widened, brightened. 'Really?'

'I'd love it.' He would too. 'My business is doing brilliantly, and I'm proud of it, but it's just something to fill in the time. I can hire a manager to take over operations, or even take on a partner. I might do the odd bit of consultancy work, just to keep my hand in, but building a family with you, Caro, is what I really want to do.'

She smiled back at him with a mistiness that had him throwing his head back and laughing for the sheer joy of it. 'We both have more money than either one of us will ever conceivably need. We can hire all the help we need or want—housekeepers, nannies, gardeners.'

Her eyes shone so bright they made him feel he was at the centre of the universe.

'Would you like to remain in London?' He didn't care *where* they lived.

'Oh! I hadn't thought about it. I love London, but I'm sure I'd love Australia too, and—'

'It's just—' he glanced around '—this house is huge. If we stayed here then maybe, down the track, we could think about fostering kids in need.'

He'd barely finished before she threw her arms around his neck and held him tight. 'That sounds perfect—absolutely perfect! Now, as it appears you won't kiss *me*, I'll just have to kiss you instead.'

His heart expanded until he thought it would grow too big for his chest. Her lips moved to within millimetres of his—

'Darlings, there's tea and cake if you'd like some.'

With a smile that set his blood on fire, Caro eased away to glance at Barbara. 'I'd love cake, but there's some paperwork I need Jack to go over…uh…upstairs.' Taking his hand, she led him out of the room, past a bemused Barbara and up the staircase. 'Make sure you leave us some!' she shot over her shoulder.

He started to laugh when they reached her room. 'You're not fooling anyone with that story, you know.'

'I know—but you can't expect a lifetime of reserve to simply vanish overnight. And the odd polite fiction keeps the wheels turning smoothly.'

He stared at her, barely able to believe he was there with her. 'I love you, Caro. I will cherish this and keep it safe—' he opened his hand to reveal the snuffbox '—in the same way I will always cherish your heart and do all I can to keep it safe.'

Her eyes burned into his. 'I love you, Jack. I will do everything I can think of to make you happy.'

'You promise to always tell me what you want?'

She nodded and then grinned. 'Want to know what I want right now?'

His mouth dried at the look in her eyes. 'What?' he croaked.

'You,' she whispered, moving across to stand in front of him. Reaching up on tiptoe, she pressed a kiss to the corner of his mouth. 'I want *you*.'

'You have me,' he promised, his lips descending towards hers.

'Forever?'

'Forever.'

* * * * *

COMING NEXT MONTH FROM

⬥ HARLEQUIN®
™

Romance

Available March 8, 2016

#4511 THE GREEK'S READY-MADE WIFE
Brides for the Greek Tycoons
by Jennifer Faye

Tycoon Cristo needs to marry to secure a vital deal and believes that chambermaid Kyra Pappas will make the perfect convenient bride. But relationships have only ever meant heartache for these two lost hearts—together can they make their fairy-tale ending finally come true...?

#4512 CROWN PRINCE'S CHOSEN BRIDE
by Kandy Shepherd

Chef Gemma knows forever isn't possible with duty-bound Tristan—no matter how charming this crown prince is! But when Tristan throws out the royal rule book, all it takes is two little words for Gemma to get her happy-ever-after..."I do!"

#4513 BILLIONAIRE, BOSS...BRIDEGROOM?
Billionaires of London
by Kate Hardy

CEO Hugh has one rule: he never mixes business with pleasure! Until he needs a fake date and decides his quirky new graphic designer, Bella, is the perfect candidate. With Bella by his side, Hugh realizes that some rules are worth breaking, especially if it means forever with Bella. So, down on one knee, he'll prove it!

#4514 MARRIED FOR THEIR MIRACLE BABY
by Soraya Lane

Ballerina Saffron is swept off her feet by tycoon Blake Goldsmith—but she doesn't expect his proposal of a convenient marriage! Blake promises to help her fulfill her dancing dreams, except another dream comes true... she's pregnant! So what will this mean for their fake marriage?

HRLPCNM0216

LARGER-PRINT BOOKS!
GET 2 FREE LARGER-PRINT NOVELS PLUS
2 FREE GIFTS!

HARLEQUIN

Romance

From the Heart, For the Heart

YES! Please send me 2 FREE LARGER-PRINT Harlequin® Romance novels and my 2 FREE gifts (gifts are worth about $10). After receiving them, if I don't wish to receive any more books, I can return the shipping statement marked "cancel." If I don't cancel, I will receive 4 brand-new novels every month and be billed just $5.09 per book in the U.S. or $5.49 per book in Canada. That's a savings of at least 15% off the cover price! It's quite a bargain! Shipping and handling is just 50¢ per book in the U.S. and 75¢ per book in Canada.* I understand that accepting the 2 free books and gifts places me under no obligation to buy anything. I can always return a shipment and cancel at any time. Even if I never buy another book, the two free books and gifts are mine to keep forever.

119/319 HDN GHWC

Name	(PLEASE PRINT)	
Address		Apt. #
City	State/Prov.	Zip/Postal Code

Signature (if under 18, a parent or guardian must sign)

Mail to the **Reader Service:**
IN U.S.A.: P.O. Box 1867, Buffalo, NY 14240-1867
IN CANADA: P.O. Box 609, Fort Erie, Ontario L2A 5X3
Want to try two free books from another line?
Call 1-800-873-8635 or visit www.ReaderService.com.

SPECIAL EXCERPT FROM

ⓗ HARLEQUIN®

Romance

*The last thing chambermaid Kyra Pappas expects
when she enters Cristo Kiriakis's hotel suite is a
proposal! But is a marriage of convenience
enough for romantic Kyra?*

*Read on for a sneak preview of
THE GREEK'S READY-MADE WIFE,
the first in Jennifer Faye's spell-binding duet
BRIDES FOR THE GREEK TYCOONS.*

It wasn't until the waiter had placed the cupcake in front
of her that she realized there was a diamond ring sitting
atop the large dollop of frosting. The jewel was big. No,
it was huge.

Kyra gasped.

The waiter immediately backed away. Cristo moved
from his chair and retrieved the ring. What was he up to?
Was it a mistake that he was going to correct? Because no
one purchased a ring that big for someone who was just
their fake fiancée.

Cristo dropped to his knee next to her chair. Her mouth
opened but no words came out. Was he going to propose
to her? Right here? In front of everyone?

Cristo gazed into her eyes. "Kyra, you stumbled into
my life, reminding me of all that I'd been missing. You
showed me that there's more to life than business. You
make me smile. You make me laugh. I can only hope to

make you nearly as happy. Will you make me the happiest man in the world and marry me?"

The words were perfect. The sentiment was everything a woman could hope for. She knew this was where she was supposed to say *yes*, but even though her jaw moved, the words were trapped in her throat. Instead, she nodded and blinked back the involuntary rush of emotions. Someday she hoped the right guy would say those words to her and mean them.

Her eyelids fluttered closed. His smooth lips pressed to hers. He was delicious, tasting sweet like the bottle of bubbly he'd insisted on ordering. She'd thought it'd just been to celebrate their business arrangement. She had no idea it was part of this seductive proposal. This man was as dangerous to her common sense as he was delicious enough to kiss all night long.

When applause and whistles filled the restaurant, it shattered the illusion. Kyra crashed back to earth and reluctantly pulled back. Her gaze met his passion-filled eyes. He wanted her. That part couldn't be faked. So that kiss had been more than a means to prove to the world that their relationship was real. The kiss had been the heart-pounding, soul-stirring genuine article.